Celebrating the Hero

Celebrating the Hero

LYLL BECERRA de JENKINS

Lodestar Books
Dutton   New York

Library of Congress Cataloging-in-Publication Data

Jenkins, Lyll Becerra de.
  Celebrating the hero/Lyll Becerra de Jenkins.—1st ed.
    p. cm.
  Summary: After her mother's death, seventeen-year-old Camila Draper travels to Colombia to attend a ceremony honoring her late grandfather and, while trying to learn more about her mother's family, discovers some disturbing truths.
  ISBN 0-525-67399-7
  [1. Family problems—Fiction. 2. Grandfathers—Fiction. 3. Colombia—Fiction.] I. Title.
PZ7.J414Ce 1993
[Fic]—dc20   93-3860
                                                            CIP
                                                            AC

Published in the United States by Lodestar Books, an affiliate of Dutton Children's Books, a division of Penguin Books USA Inc., 375 Hudson Street, New York, New York 10014

Published simultaneously in Canada by McClelland & Stewart, Toronto

Editor: Rosemary Brosnan   Designer: Richard Granald

Printed in the U.S.A.   First Edition   10 9 8 7 6 5 4 3 2 1

for
Francesca, Marcela, and Alexandra
and for
Teresa and Gabriela

Celebrating the Hero

1

"You have a letter from South America, honey!" Irma calls. Every afternoon she receives me with a piece of news. Her purpose is to create a momentary animation that would dissipate my somber mood as I come into the house, empty now of Matesa, the name I often used to call Mama.

I drop my leather bag that holds my books onto the table in the foyer. Then I walk into the kitchen first, along the hall, and in and out of the rooms. Every day I go through this same tour, as if I am convincing myself that my mother is waiting for me somewhere in the house. Finally I step out to the terrace, where I look at the garden, a place I now avoid.

"Look at the pretty flowers," Irma calls, pointing at a crystal vase in the dining room filled with plastic flowers. She's the housekeeper. My father feels I need a companion now. I turn my head, pretending I'm obeying her suggestion. Instead, I see the fresh roses from our garden Mama used to arrange in vases around the house this time of the year.

"The stamps on your letter are so pretty."

"Are they?" I ask mechanically as I go on in my senseless searching for images of the past. But all visions of Matesa have fused into one: her figure bending over the bush of red roses that afternoon last October, while my voice went on calling in vain, "Mama, Mama."

I approach the kitchen desk, where Irma puts the mail. There, separated from the other letters, I see my name, *Señorita Camila Draper,* on the envelope with the colorful stamps: Simón Bolívar in his red military uniform.

My suspicion that the letter from South America was from Uncle Victor or one of my cousins repeating their invitation for me to spend this summer in Bogotá with them vanishes as I look at the handwriting: Consonants and vowels are so embellished, the letters seem drawn rather than written. Pale and dark lines alternate, each word ending with an exaggerated bow. The letters curl and twist, resembling Irma's fake flowers. I slip the envelope into my skirt pocket, then pick up my leather bag in the foyer and walk up the stairs to my room, closing the door.

I open the envelope, grateful that the letter, which is written in Spanish, of course, has been typed. It's an official communication from the mayor of San Javier, my mother's town in the state of Santander, Colombia.

Dear Señorita Camila Draper: It's my pleasure to invite you to attend the ceremony that San Javier has organized to honor the memory of Don Pachito Zamora, Illustrious Son of this town.

As I go on reading, I find myself translating the letter into English automatically. I don't like their calling him Don Pachito. Francisco Zamora, my grandfather's name, has the resonance of a poem in my ears. But I like the term *Illustrious Son*. *"Hijo Ilustre,"* I repeat to myself, wondering why the two words, which have dignity in Spanish, turn trite in English. I continue reading:

It's our hope that you, his American granddaughter, will join your uncle, Doctor Victor Zamora, and his family, who will be here in San Javier for this important occasion.

The letter goes on, explaining that the house where

Don Pachito lived and died, and where his two children Victor and María Teresa were born,

is being prepared to receive the family. The homage will consist of the placing of a marble pillar with my grandfather's name in the plaza of San Javier during the last weekend of July.

It's our hope that you'll be one of us on that day when we will all gather under the blue sky of San Javier, where Don Pachito's eyes saw the first light and the last shadows.

The letter fills me with pride. Also with sadness. How excited Mama would have been! Often, the two of us talked about going together to San Javier. Yet I know that had Matesa been alive, I would have made fun of the handwriting on the envelope and of the poetic attempt in the letter's closing. I would have probably said, "I can't go, Matesa," thinking of my own summer plans. Now I hear my voice murmuring, "I'll go, Mama. I'll be in San Javier that day."

I call my father to tell him about the invitation. I'm sure he'll be pleased to hear that I am anxious to go to San

Javier. He often says, "This is what Matesa wants," and "This is how your mother feels about this." Papa still speaks as if his wife were alive, only somewhere in another room of the house.

Vivian, his secretary, tells me that he just went into a meeting. "But I'll find a way to let him know that you want to talk to him, Camila."

Like the neighbors, Vivian treats me with special deference, the sympathy inspired by a girl who has lost her mother unexpectedly. It's the warm tone people use that often brings tears to my eyes.

A moment later, when my father calls, I read the letter in Spanish, changing and skipping a few words, instinctively adapting the phrases to a more casual American style, as Matesa would have done. I omit the last lines about the "blue sky" and "the first light and the last shadows."

I wait for his comments, wondering about his long silence. Finally, he says, "Do you think you should go, Camila?"

"But of course, Dad, I should go!"

I am anxious to hear "This is what your mother wants." Instead, he tells me, "We'll discuss it when I get home."

I'm silent for a moment. Then I say, "Dad, you'll be in San Javier for the ceremony, won't you? Matesa wants you there that day."

"I'll be there, Camila!"

❦ 2 ❦

At the desk in Barranquilla, a pretty woman with a voluminous mane of shiny black hair informs me that the national airline with my reservation for Bogotá has been on strike since midnight.

"How can I reach San Javier?" I ask, surprised at my question, which should have been "How can I be in Bogotá today?"

"San Javier? Where's that?" the pretty woman mutters, although her attention is on one of her nails, which has apparently just broken. *"Un momentico,"* she says, rushing away, perhaps to find a file.

A man behind the desk who has just finished helping a couple addresses me. "There are no planes traveling directly to San Javier, señorita." I could fly to Bucaramanga, the capital city of the state of Santander, in an airtaxi, he explains. From there I could rent a car. "However, I don't advise you to do it, señorita—"

"Why?"

"Muy peligroso—very dangerous," he says.

The voice of a woman in line behind me repeats, *"Muy peligroso."*

5

"*Un momentico,*" the man begs as someone calls him from the back of the office. He rushes away. I stand there, waiting. Perhaps because of the early hour, there's not a crowd yet. Those who are there all seem to know what to do: Some walk to the restaurant to have breakfast; others sit or stand reading newspapers or are involved in conversations. I feel as if I am the only one who doesn't know what to do. My indecision must show on my face. A woman nearby says, "Don't worry. There are many other flights, not big planes, but little ones . . . don't worry."

I turn, explaining briefly that my family is waiting, that it is urgent for me to be in San Javier.

"Are you American?" the woman asks. She's wearing a pink, unclean turban and carries in her hand a dirty canvas bag, the contents of which she has covered with a colorful bandana.

"I am half—yes, I am American."

"How come your Spanish is so good?"

" *Sí, sí,* very good," confirms a thin young man wearing a baseball cap. An older woman by his side, thinner than he, repeats, "*Sí, muy bueno.*"

The airline employee is back, apologizing. Only he and two other people are answering questions today. "The strike, you see," he explains.

The girl with the broken nail is also back. She darts a resentful glance at me, who apparently should have waited until she solved her nail crisis.

An international plane to Ecuador via Barranquilla and Bogotá is about to land, the man explains. He's almost sure he'll find a place for me there. He brings out a computer sheet. "Another option is to travel in one of the airtaxis to Bucaramanga. From there you could catch one of the buses that goes to San Javier."

"Airtaxi . . ." I murmur, thinking about my father's admonition, "Don't take risks, Camila." I ask, "Are airtaxis like regular planes? Are they, I mean . . ." I finish my question in my mind: Are airtaxis safe?

"Airtaxis are dependable, señorita," he answers, guessing my question.

"Today, with the strike, they'll be like flies," someone shouts. The prospect of being in San Javier by myself is too strong a temptation. "And in Bucaramanga—can I rent a car there?"

"I told you, señorita: It's a risk—unless you're with someone else?"

"I'm all alone."

"Muy peligroso," several answer in unison.

I turn. A small gathering is at my back. None of them look like passengers waiting for their turn.

"A bus is better," says the airline attendant.

"No, no, Señor Domingo, a bus is worse," a little man, holding a broom and with a pencil above his ear, which seems bigger than his face, says. He's clearly one of the janitors at the airport. He has begun a story about the fate of a few bus passengers last week, a horrible story I don't want to hear. The others are all asking him to shut his mouth.

I interrupt, "What is not dangerous?"

Everyone, including the company employee, bursts out laughing.

7

"Everything . . . These days everything is dangerous in this country of ours. *Todo*," answers a man smoking a cigar, standing away from the others. He alone is not laughing, his expression as solemn as his voice.

A crowd is coming into the airport. An international flight, announced a moment before, has landed.

"I'll take a ticket, please, for the airtaxi to Bucaramanga," I say in a hushed voice, aware of a change in my breathing for falling into a temptation I cannot resist.

"One will be leaving shortly, ten forty-five, all right?" the airline employee asks, glancing at his wristwatch.

After the man gives me the ticket at last, I rush to call Uncle Victor. The woman with the turban, the janitor, the thin couple, and the man with the cigar follow me. "All alone," I hear one of the men saying, then the woman with the turban adding, *"Pobrecita."*

From inside the phone booth, I look at the strange group. I'm sure that none of them is there to catch a plane. They are dressed as the janitor is, in wrinkled shirts and work pants. The woman with the turban looks like a bag lady from the streets of New York. The thin couple is smoking a cigarette between themselves. He takes a puff and gives it to her; then, after she takes her turn, she puts it in his mouth delicately, gently, with a devotion that makes me think that they are exchanging kisses rather than nicotine. They are all at the airport, I say to myself, because here they feel a part of the crowd. Perhaps they make themselves believe they are also travelers, flying to a distant land . . . some place of their dreams. Do they expect something from me? I wonder. I want to do the right thing. They gave me support in my momentary panic.

The maid in Bogotá finally answers the telephone. "Doctor Victor is at the hospital and the señora . . ." She goes on and on explaining what every member of the family is doing that morning. "Ah, *sí*, señorita, I know they are all very happy expecting you today and—"

I manage to interrupt at last. "Tell them I am fine, not to worry. Tell Uncle Victor I'll be in touch with him soon, tonight."

I am panting as I get out of the phone booth. I did not lie on the telephone, nor did I say the truth. I look around. My friends are nowhere. Maybe it's someone else's turn to receive their support, I tell myself. I move about until I find a place to sit and wait. On a table nearby there are magazines and newspapers, but I don't bother. The idea of being in San Javier alone ahead of time, of finding someone who remembers Grandfather and would speak to me about him fills me with exhilaration. To be there, to remember . . . To remember? I correct myself, feeling indeed as if I'm returning to San Javier, rather than going for the first time.

I never met my grandfather, yet his presence while I was growing up was constant. "You were born on the first anniversary of his death, Camila, the same week of the same month," Matesa often said. She'd pause, her dark eyes looking at me intently, as if urging me to reflect on the significance of my arrival in the world, and my grandfather's departure from it, in "the same week of the same month."

9

The first stories I heard as a child were about my grandfather. At fourteen, he had been sent by his family to buy a stallion for the farm. "He was the only boy and had two sisters. The trail to his destination in Orocué led through hostile terrain crossed by turbulent rivers and plagued by bandits. Your grandfather was robbed of his money and his horse, but he made it by foot to the farm of the stallions."

It was not so much the stories themselves that I found intriguing. It was the music of Mama's voice telling them in Spanish. Grandfather had become the owner of the best horses in the region—Caracol, Relámpago, Colibrí. His horses' names brought to my mind the vision of Grandfather galloping over the plains of Santander, where in my imagination every night was moonlit. I would go to sleep pronouncing the names, rolling the words in my mouth as if they were caramels. So often had I heard the story of Matesa going to Sunday Mass, holding her father's hand, that in my memory I myself was the child with the frilly dress and the butterfly bow on my hair, entering the church of San Javier, holding the hand of Francisco Zamora, who was dressed in a white linen suit and panama hat.

"The background of the main altar was a picture of God, a colossal, white-bearded face emerging from a tempestuous sky crossed by lightning, a frowning God of fiery eyes, so terrifying an image I kept my head bowed for the duration of the Mass." I would dream about a flaming sky from which a giant man dressed in white descended slowly, stepping over hills and trees, approaching, his hand extended toward me, his granddaughter. Hearing the description of my recurring dream, Mama would rectify, "Your grandfather was not a big man, Camila. *Era un hombre pequeño.*"

A man shouting against the strike interrupts my recollections. Why was he not informed? he demands, walking away, waving his arms. A woman and several children carrying suitcases and packages rush to follow him.

I remember that as I grew up, the stories about my grandfather slowly began to change. I was somewhat unhappy with the grandfather of Matesa's new stories, the angry man who belted his son, Victor, "because he wouldn't bring his father his cigar and newspaper on time," just as he himself, Grandfather, had been punished, for this was "how boys grew up to be *hombres.*" I was uncertain of my grandfather, who forced his family to live in monastic abstinence so that he could donate the house that became the first school in San Javier. What disturbed me more was that I had lost the image of my grandfather. I was no longer dreaming of the giant approaching, his hand extended toward me. Was Mama perhaps giving me the knowledge of my grandfather like lessons at school—textbooks that change as education advances? I often wondered.

One night I had a dream I have never forgotten. A little, ugly man in the center of a stage was moving his hands up and down, tossing objects I couldn't make out into space, retrieving them again in the air. At first I didn't recognize the man. Then with a sadness I could feel in my dream, I realized the ugly little man was my grandfather, "the *hombre pequeño*" that Matesa had described. That was the last time I dreamed about my grandfather.

"Tell me something nice about Grandfather, Mama," I'd ask from time to time.

"He played the mandolin. Your grandfather composed songs about valiant men whose pride was to defend the honor of their land and their women."

"Did he compose love songs?"

"Love, as you mean it, I don't know. He composed a tender song for Victor and me."

"Do you remember it? Would you sing it for me?"

"It brings back so many memories—my childhood, Victor's." But she walked to the piano and played a simple, repetitive melody for a while. Then in her lovely contralto voice she sang, *"Porque mi camino es corto y estrecho . . ."*

I translated the song into English and we would often sing it together in Spanish or English.

> *"Because my road is short and narrow*
> *And yours so wide, so clear*
> *Let me tell you my memories*
> *Let me listen to your dreams."*

"You rarely speak about Grandmother. Why?" I'd often burst out.

"My mother suffered from nerves. She needed to be alone. Papa would take Victor and me on trips or would send us away." Matesa would utter the words quickly, yet reluctantly, like a child repeating a difficult lesson she had been forced to memorize.

12

Slowly I began to avoid Matesa's stories. I felt as if my mother's voice, her constant telling about San Javier, was a loud noise interrupting my own inner rhythms, as intrusive as a hand sweeping away fragments of my own memories.

One Sunday, after we said good-bye to Papa, who was going on a business trip, Matesa and I sat in the porch. She began, "Once my father—"

I interrupted, "Please, let's talk about something else, Mama. So many stories! Sometimes I don't know which are your stories and which are my own." That Sunday has remained vivid in my mind.

The voice in the loudspeaker is calling my airtaxi flight. A moment later, as I walk in line with other passengers, checking my travel documents, I hear "*Buen víaje, seño-rita.*" I turn and see the woman with the turban. She's explaining to everyone around about me. "She's a gringa, but she speaks Spanish. She's all alone." She punctuates the last word with a noisy sigh. I accelerate my step. At the door of the tiny plane, I pause. There, amidst the crowd that is saying good-bye to friends and relatives, I see the thin man with his companion and the one with the cigar. They are all waving to me. I remain there for an instant with my fluttering hand, until I realize that I am acting as if I were a local beauty queen waving to her fans.

The tiny plane sways and jerks like a kite. I close my eyes while I think of the time Mama and I went to visit Uncle Victor and his family in Bogotá. I had simultaneously loved and hated being there. I can still see myself with my twin cousins, my uncle, and Aunt Natalia. There were also daily visits of distant relatives anxious to see Mama and meet me, "La Gringuita," as they called me. "Do you feel American . . . no? Colombian . . . yes?" "Wouldn't you prefer living here, Camila?" Everyone had a question for me. No one, however, paused long enough to hear what I said. I ended up mumbling my own answers to myself. After a week, it had seemed to me that they all had been trained to speak at the same time, to raise their voices in unison. They were like a chorus with an invisible conductor commanding them to keep up the high volume and the effusiveness.

One evening after dinner, I excused myself and escaped to bed early. Just when I was about to turn off the lamp, Mama walked in. Was I not feeling well? she wanted to know. I said I was just tired. I avoided meeting her eyes, thinking that Matesa was probably embarrassed, recalling what she had so often told me about the stimulating dialogues, the wonderful conversations, "the art of sitting down to exchange thoughts and ideas that is still cultivated in my country."

"Your cousins were wondering if perhaps you're bored with them."

"Of course not; I like being here."

"I knew it. I knew you'd love it here, Camila," Mama said, kissing me good-night. At the door she turned to say, "You probably thought I was exaggerating, didn't you?"

Yet on the plane returning to Connecticut I surprised myself by crying, feeling that something of myself was remaining forever in my mother's land. For the first time I understood that what matters is not how things happen but the way people find a way to one's heart, becoming a part of one's life. That day I knew I would be telling stories to my friends, that, like my mother, I also one day would be repeating to my children, "In Colombia . . ."

3

I have been on the bus on my way to San Javier for almost two hours. "We'll be arriving around four-thirty . . . if everything goes all right," says the driver. He's a young man with red hair and a red moustache. Matesa told me once that the first colonizers of Santander were Dutch. The driver has been giving reports periodically, always including a word or a sentence to create tension. "If we reach Posada Los Chulos, we'll be all right," he shouted a moment before. He keeps observing me through the mirror in front of him. I have put my hair up, seeking a mature look. Nothing in the way he glances at me makes me distrustful. I am not even worried at the sight of the pistol he's carrying under his lightweight jacket. My excitement about being in San Javier by myself leaves no space for other feelings.

There are only a few passengers. A well-dressed, middle-aged couple; a man reading the newspaper with concentration; two women who are on the same bench chatting in low voices, one with a small child on her lap; and a campesino tightly embracing his traditional *mochila*, a woven bag. Every time the bus driver shouts a report I can feel a wave of alarm sweeping throughout each one of us. The bus stops in the middle of nowhere. A man and a boy emerge from the trees along the road. Behind them several women appear, wearing bright cotton dresses and white straw hats typical of the campesinos in this region. They climb up into the bus, greeting Señor Pinzón, the driver. Just as the bus is about to continue, a man outside shouts, "Wait, Wait!" Two peasants approach, bringing into the bus a strong smell of alcohol. Both have machetes hanging from their belts. The driver stares at them, shaking his head in disapproval. I can't help noticing the contrast these peasants make with the Andean campesinos whom I saw on my first trip, the stooped figures in dark clothes and ponchos who bow repeatedly, moving about in silence. I recall my mother saying, "Observe these campesinos, Camila. Every one of their gestures is like an apology, as if their existence is an unwelcome intrusion on the rest of the world." The peasants from this region keep their heads up, speak in loud voices, and wear a kind of haughtiness on their faces.

Occasionally, a turbid river comes into view. Naked children are bathing and running around while women wash clothes, rubbing them against the stones. I doze on and off until the bus stops abruptly. I see a police car with two officers inside. "Everything all right?" one of them asks. Everyone in the bus, myself included, assents with our heads. The driver takes a long time to answer. "So far . . ." he says at last, perhaps not to break the tension of his reports. The bus proceeds downhill along a narrow road of red earth that goes around and around in its descent, like a spiral orange peel. The well-dressed couple is smiling and talking to each other.

"That's San Javier, señorita." The driver turns to me.

"I see. *Gracias,*" I reply with enthusiasm. From the hill the town looks larger than I had expected. I see buildings, pretty houses with gardens, a stadium or bullfight ring, a huge stone construction with towers on the downhill looking like a castle. To my left there are tombs, white wooden crosses sloping down toward the village. San Javier Cemetery, where Grandfather rests, I think, but I look away quickly, telling myself that I'm here to find out about my grandfather when he was alive.

"We made it!" the driver says, knocking on the bus roof. Anyone would believe he means that the old, dusty, noisy bus has behaved, but I know, of course, that in the Colombia of today he means that he did not have to use his pistol, that we made it to our destination alive.

The bus is entering the plaza. "I am in San Javier, I am in San Javier," the beating of my heart seems to repeat. A crowd is waiting for the bus, which brings mail, packages, and newspapers. A boy unloads them from the back. The driver has already jumped out. He is shouting names as he delivers parcels and envelopes to the men and women dashing to get them as they are called.

I search for my suitcase.

"Is this the suitcase of the foreign señorita?" a boy asks.

"That's it," the driver answers, instructing the boy to carry it.

Thanking the man, I begin following the boy. Three taxis are parked in front of an attractive white stone house enclosed by an ornamental iron fence. A board hanging from the balcony reads HOTEL EL REGAZO.

"I'm not going to the hotel," I explain, as the boy moves ahead without asking questions.

"I know; you're going to the house of Don Pachito in Calle de Los Naranjos."

"How do you know?"

"My grandma recognized you when you came out of the bus and Señor Pinzón called me to help you. She said you're Don Pachito's daughter."

"I am his granddaughter."

The boy shrugs his shoulders, as if to say, "Same thing."

"What's your name?" I ask, following him.

"Tomás, *su servidor.*"

I don't recognize anything in spite of Matesa's repeated descriptions. A few modern buildings are around the plaza. There's a restaurant with red and white awnings and tables on the sidewalk. One table is occupied by two men. The rest of the houses are old—white stone and tile roof homes, contrasting with the modern buildings. The dark, almost black, stone church sits on a high terrace. But I recognize the oak trees, "each one with a bench under its shade." The town looks as if it's reluctant to embrace its own character, as if half of it wants to remain as it had been from the beginning, while the other half wants to become modern. I can sense the disparity, even in the loud music that is coming from the restaurant, a song I like. "But not here," I murmur to myself. Gato Barbieri's "Emiliano Zapata" in the plaza of San Javier seems to me an intrusion.

19

"You don't need a taxi." The boy pauses as he sees me standing there, looking around. "They charge a lot of money, and your house is nearby. Just walk where I walk."

"I will, Tomás, thank you."

He turns, smiling, as I call his name.

The crowd that waited for the mail and packages has dispersed. The bus is now being parked in front of a white wall with a door and a high, square window—probably the town's tavern. The wall is covered with graffiti.

I give a start as I now hear the church bells tolling energetically, infusing electricity to the plaza. A man's guffaw reverberates almost as loudly. I feel shy. Could it be—are the bells ringing in my honor? I wonder absurdly. Tomás, standing at the corner, waits. I move faster. "Tomás, why are the church bells ringing?"

"*Nada,*" he says, placing the suitcase on the ground, slapping the air. "It's Don Cristóbal, the sacristan. He gets bored and up he goes to make noise. Many don't like it. And when he's drunk"—Tomás lets out a short whistle—"when he's drunk, he rings the bells like *loco* in the middle of the night."

"What about the priest, doesn't he—?"

"Padre Roque is as deaf as a wall." The boy picks up the suitcase and we turn the corner away from the plaza. The trees at either side of the narrow street bow to one another, fanning the air, which feels cooler than the plaza's. The solid stone houses display baskets of red, white, and pink geraniums in their windows. There's a strong aroma of orange blossoms.

"Is this the street?"

"Yes, señorita, this is la Calle de los Naranjos," Tomás answers.

As I approach the house, I hear my mother's description. "Closing the block, into a dead-end street was our house, a gray stone house, enclosed by a black wrought iron gate that could be opened from outside. The two narrow alleys at either side were used by the pedestrians living on the street who wanted a shortcut to the church and the market. At the end of the backyard sat a solitary oak tree."

There are no plants or flowers at the windows, only a privet hedge outside the gate. The facade is austere. There seems to be an effort in its simplicity, the straight lines of the door and windows, its total absence of adornments. The word *masculine* comes to my mind. A gentlemanly house, I decide. I'm only disappointed that the street has been paved. I recall Matesa's description of how at night she could hear the clatter of her father's horse on the cobblestone street. "But that was when I was a small child, that was *before* . . ." In her last year Mama would emphasize that word. "*Before* what, Mama?" I murmur now as if she's here with me, as if now I'm ready to listen to what I stopped her from telling.

4

A girl with a ponytail, wearing a blue uniform, opens the door, looking at me inquiringly.

"I am Don Francisco's granddaughter." Before I finish introducing myself, the girl is uttering exclamations. "We were not expecting . . ." She covers her mouth with one hand, her eyes popping out. "We thought it was . . . Nobody told us . . ." She leaves all her sentences incomplete. Finally, taking her hand from her mouth, she says, "Welcome, señorita."

"I know I am not supposed to be here until Friday; you must forgive me." I explain briefly about the airline strike. Halfway into the entrance hall, seeing the girl ahead of me with my suitcase, I remember the boy. "Tomás!" I run to the door shouting his name, but there's no trace of him. "I didn't give him anything—"

"Don't worry, señorita, he didn't do it for the money. My name is Pepa, but everyone calls me Pepita."

An older woman standing at the end of the entrance hall is peering at me. She's also wearing a blue uniform. In her arms she has a load of bed linen. I am interrupting the

22

women, who are in the midst of preparing the house for Friday's arrival. "I'm sorry," I begin.

"Come in, come in. You're the American señorita, the daughter of Señora María Teresa. I'm Josefa." She stretches a hand from under the load of linen.

"You knew my mother?"

"When she was young . . . when I myself was also a girl. You see, my mother was in the service of this house since she herself was almost a child. Doctor Victor gave instructions to give you the best room. 'The best room is for my niece Camila,' that's what he ordered. And you know? It's the only room that is ready. We didn't know you were coming. Please, señorita." She beckons me to enter.

We step into an open patio of shiny black and white tiles. Earthen pots with ferns and other plants with exotic, twinkling leaves are placed around the patio. A couple of paint cans sit at the side of the hall adjacent to the patio. "I am so happy to be here! You see, my mother told me so much about this place. I wanted to be ahead of everyone to see." I finally become aware that I have been raising my voice higher and higher with each word. I am overwhelmed by a feeling of euphoria. "Well, I promise not to be in your way," I say, lowering my tone. A double door of cherry wood, resembling the portico of a chapel, is still shining with fresh varnish.

Pepita has disappeared with the suitcase.

"This way, Señorita Camila," Josefa calls. "The bathroom is at the end of the house, in the third patio. Sometimes it gets chilly at night, and who wants to walk all the way. But there are enough chamber pots and hot water in every room." She enters, moving to a corner, opening a door that looks like a closet but is a tiny space with a basin, a mirror, and towels. "I hope you'll be comfortable here, señorita."

The large room with a high ceiling has a double bed and an enormous old-fashioned armoire of dark wood, like the freshly varnished door in the first hall. A rectangular window the width of the bed is set high on the wall. There's a rocking chair and a tiny table nearby with a bowl of *granadillas,* a local fruit. In a corner is a square, solid basket, the hamper. The brand-new white wrought iron dressing table and matching stool don't belong with the rest of the furniture. They were probably added at the last moment for my comfort, I conclude.

A multitude of pictures fills one of the walls. Some are large; most are postcard size. A few have been arranged inside a large single frame.

"Just as I recall it," I murmur.

Josefa, who is closing the white curtains on the window, turns sharply. "But you—you haven't been here, señorita."

"I have . . . in a way. Only this picture . . ." I'm looking at a portrait of a woman with dark, curly hair. She's sitting on a high stool and is inclined as if she's about to whisper a secret, her long, beautiful hand on her chin.

"That's your grandmother, Doña Adelaida. The portrait belongs to the doctor, your uncle. He ordered us to place it here for the time being."

It's the first time I see a clear picture of my grandmother. Matesa had one on her dressing table showing a thin, tall woman coming out of church, wearing a hat

24

that shadowed her face. Josefa and I are both silent, look-ing at the portrait. There's something mischievous in the delicate face of the young Adelaida, as if she's laughing at the photographer, who had probably been repeating, "More to the left, a little more. Keep your hand there; look at the camera." The large, dark eyes, the mouth, the whole face are vivacious, exuberant. Like a flower, a fruit, I say to myself.

"Are you thirsty, hungry? What may I offer you?" Josefa's voice interrupts my thoughts.

"Nothing, Josefa, maybe later. I'd like to rest?" I'm anx-ious to be alone in the room.

Josefa remains there for a moment, looking around her, checking the room.

Josefa's polite expression is fixed on her face like a mask. I recall my mother telling about humble women she had known in Colombia who were fearful of expressing anger or sadness.

"Let me know if you need something, señorita." The woman walks out at last.

Even the smell of the room, a mixture of lumber and or-ange blossoms, contributes to my joy. I take off my cardi-gan, tossing it over the hamper, then wrap my arms around myself, feeling embraced by the room, the whole house. Here I am, Camila Draper, with all my mother's family, my ancestors. I swirl, surprising myself, as if someone—my grandfather?—is giving me a spin, saying, "Let me look at you, Camila." I feel a warmth on my shoulder—the light weight of Mama's hand, I say to my-self. "I'm so glad, so glad to be here." I close my eyes and see Matesa's dark, luminous eyes gazing at me. "I'm so glad to be here," I repeat to her. Slowly, intently, I absorb every object in the room—to preserve it all, to carry it with me as vividly as I see it now. I approach the wall to see the small pictures better. One shows a group of men with panama hats, playing guitars. A man in the center of the group has a different instrument, a mandolin. "My grandfather!" I burst out. He looks very small. *"El era pequeño,"* I hear Mama's soft voice. They are all short men. A thought steals into my mind: Handsome, well-proportioned dwarfs. I cover my mouth, laughing. Grandfather's expression is somewhat stern, contrasting with the smiling faces of the other men.

One picture shows couples dancing under a large tree. Apart from them a little girl with short, straight hair and bangs is holding her skirt, dancing by herself. There are several pictures of women and men on horses, the women riding sidesaddle. It's clear that most of the photos were taken on picnics. "It was on these social occasions that men and women fell in love. But I didn't participate in any of San Javier's social life, not even as a teenager. Papa was always sending me away," Matesa often said.

In one of the larger photos a woman in a white dress has separated herself from the group of men and women, who are all laughing, posing for the photographer, their eyes on the camera. The woman's face is half turned, as she extends a protective hand to a little girl with bangs and a ribbon like a butterfly on her hair, who is balancing herself on a rock nearby. The child, I know, is Matesa, yet it's the woman who attracts me. Why is she isolated from the others? What is evocative and vibrant in the portrait of my grandmother is listless and joyless in this small photo. Her eyes, looking up at the child on the rock, can be seen clearly in the picture. Under my fixed gaze, they seem to acquire the brilliance of eyes with tears. I shake my head to dispel my supposition. Mama used to compare my imagination with a galloping horse. But there's so little I know about my grandmother Adelaida. Was it enough for me to learn that she suffered from nervous breakdowns—enough for my mother to tell me no more? Did I believe that Grandmother Adelaida was mute and still, an ornament in the house? That she was like the lonely oak in the backyard? "She *prayed* and she *sang*," Matesa said once. I move around the room repeating the two words, which suddenly seem to me so foreboding. Were praying and singing the refuges where Grandmother escaped? I hug myself, eager to bring back my feelings of elation.

I hear a commotion coming from the front door. Can it be that Uncle Victor has arrived? Running feet approach. "Señorita, you have a visitor," Pepita calls from outside the door. *"Una persona importante."*

"Who?" I ask, opening the door.

"La Primera Autoridad."

"The First Authority—who's that? How does he know I am here?"

"He knows everything," Pepita intones. "Please, señorita, he's waiting," the girl urges, her eyes widening.

"All right, Pepita. I'll be out shortly." I close the door, inspecting my blouse, deciding against changing it. Seeing my wrinkled clothes, the First Authority will conclude that I'm tired and anxious to be left alone, I tell myself. I wash my hands in the basin, smooth my hair, and walk out, sensing, as I move along the hall, that somehow the visitor has spoiled the intimacy, the atmosphere of the past that I so strongly felt when I walked in.

5

The visitor is standing by the door of what is probably the living room. He's a pale, tall man with a mouth of thick pink, almost red lips that makes me think of a clown. I'm disappointed to see that he's young, too young to have been acquainted with my grandfather.

He rushes toward me. "A pleasure meeting you, Señorita Draper. I'm Enrique Lozano."

"*Mucho gusto,*" I say, recognizing his name immediately. He is the person who signed the letter inviting me to attend the tribute for Grandfather.

"Had I known you were arriving today, I would have sent someone, or I myself would have traveled to Bucaramanga with Yolanda, my wife, to drive you here. My understanding was that you were coming with your uncle and his family on Friday."

"It was planned that way, yes, but—things worked out differently. And, you see, I wanted to be in San Javier ahead of . . . I'd like to find someone who knew my grandfather and would tell me about him."

"Very interesting, very interesting." He smiles as if amused by my reason to come ahead of the others. His

29

eyes are on the paint cans against the wall. "I'm afraid, Señorita Draper, that the house is still not ready. I hope you'll be comfortable."

"I'm so pleased to be here, to have my grandparents' bedroom."

"Don Pachito's bedroom," he corrects. "Everything, of course, has been changed."

"Changed?" My voice comes out too loud.

"Remodeled," he quickly adds. "Let me explain. The house was rather neglected since the death of Señora Chinca two years ago, although Josefa comes every week to check on things and your uncle has been here a couple of times. I understand he's anxious to make some improvements. He talked to a realtor and is waiting for you and your father, since you're now the other owner, to make a final decision." Lowering his voice, he says, "I don't think the doctor is very fond of San Javier."

"He isn't?"

"I don't know, maybe sad memories. We all have them, don't we?" he says, looking away, taking a step toward the hall. "I want to show you something, Señorita Camila. I'd like to hear your opinion." He moves ahead of me to the side of the hall toward the impressive door with fresh varnish. Pushing it softly, he gestures for me to walk in first. I enter a dark, wood-paneled room with a long table and two benches at either side of it. At the head of the table is a stately armchair. The centerpiece is an earthenware jug, egg-shaped at the bottom, narrowing at the top like the neck of a heron. The dining room resembles that of a monastery. Lozano is observing me intently, waiting for me to say something.

"The dining room," I say foolishly. "Very—"

"You haven't noticed the main thing in the room, señorita." He's pointing at the only picture on the walls. Indeed, I have not seen the portrait, which is as dark as the wall.

"You recognize him, of course. Your mother must have shown you pictures."

The man in the portrait is familiar and a stranger at the same time. "Grandfather?" I ask at last. I feel uneasy looking at the face. The lower lip twists and the eyes are like two slits, as if the artist had pushed a knife to make the two incisions, which he then covered with a pair of frameless glasses, intensifying the harshness of the countenance. At last I say, "I don't recognize my grandfather. In the portrait we have at home, he has a noble face. And the glasses—why? In all the pictures and in descriptions from my mother, she never told me that he wore glasses."

"Ah, sí, the glasses. Well, I must confess"—he licks his pink, fleshy lips—"the glasses were my idea. I thought they gave Don Pachito a touch of distinction. Let me explain, señorita." He pauses, regarding me condescendingly. His hand moves as if he's about to pat my head, this foolish young girl's head, whose abrupt frankness has probably offended him. "There was a shoe box with pictures up on the second floor." He points at the ceiling. "I took the liberty of going through them, selected the most appropriate photo, and gave it to one of our local artists.

31

Frankly, I think it is a good portrait of your grandfather." He looks at me intently.

I look away.

"Let me tell you, señorita. It hasn't been easy to organize this event in his honor. The people of San Javier are— what shall I say? They are ungrateful. Only a handful remember your grandfather. There have been a few who asked, 'Pachito who?' 'Don Francisco Zamora,' I said, 'the man who built the first school and hospital, the person who traveled to the capital every time there was a local crisis. Don Pachito,' I said, 'he who, before dying, donated the municipal gymnasium.' " His voice has taken the sing-song tone of a speech. "But they all remember him for the other thing, ah, yes, for *that* their memory of Francisco Zamora remains clear."

"The other thing? What was the— For what do they remember my grandfather?"

Lozano frowns, shakes his head, then begins to walk out.

"I want to know that *thing* for which my grandfather is remembered, Señor Lozano, please?" I'm aware of my high-pitched voice.

"Well, very simply, señorita, like every man, your grandfather had enemies."

Pepita is standing outside the door with a tray, two glasses, and a jug. Her eyes are lifted to the First Authority.

"Before I forget—you're having dinner with us," he says.

"When—tonight?" My immediate impulse is to say no, to explain that I'm tired and would like to be by myself. The truth is that I have made plans to walk around the town, to find someone who would tell me about my mother when she was a girl and about my grandfather. Then I recall what my father said: "Be careful, Camila; don't forget the cultural differences. Their sensibilities are easily hurt. At every instant, pause and think what Matesa would do or say. In San Javier you'll be representing your mother." Smiling, I thank him for the invitation.

We are now in the living room, which I'm seeing for the first time. It's a rather small room with two sofas and three armchairs, all in solid beige. The only colors are provided by an outstanding South American rug with Indian motifs. Two oval mirrors on opposite walls face each other.

Pepita is pouring *curuba* juice, offering the first glass to the *Primera Autoridad*.

"Can you tell me of anyone who was a friend of my grandfather and is still alive?"

Señor Lozano taps his lips with his index finger repeatedly as he's thinking. "Don Teodoro Espinoza," he says after a moment. "Yes . . . he was Don Pachito's close friend. He lives in one of the houses by the river with his daughter, an old maid." No sooner does he say it than he begins shaking his head. "No, no; please forget it. I shouldn't expose you to them. Both the old man and his daughter are known for their unsociability, their despotic manners. They live like hermits and want to be left alone."

A quick tapping of heels advances along the entrance hall as he's saying the last sentence. Smiling, taking a step toward the door, he explains, "My wife, Yolanda."

An attractive young woman puts her face through the door. "May I interrupt?"

He takes her by the arm and makes the introductions. Like him, she's tall and trim. She's wearing a light yellow pantsuit, the same color as the roses she carries in one arm and offers to me.

"Señorita—may I call you Camila?" he asks, offering his wife his unfinished glass of juice. "Camila was asking me if I know anyone in town who is still alive who was a friend of Don Pachito."

"A friend? Still alive . . . Of course, Padre Roque, the priest."

"Indeed. Why didn't I think of him? He's very old. We have a saying in San Javier that Padre Roque is already dead; the reason why he's still moving around is because no one has taken the trouble to bury him."

I laugh with them.

"You're coming to our house tonight. Did you mention it, Enrique?"

"Yes, thank you! Should I make an appointment with the priest before I—"

"No, no, you just go and talk to him. We're very informal here," she says.

I excuse myself and walk out to find a vase for the roses. The sky over the patio is already dark. The whole afternoon gone, I think with dismay. Pepita takes the bouquet. As I approach the living room, I hear the Lozanos deliberating in low voices. Should they wait for "the girl" and drive her to their place themselves or perhaps . . . "I have a lot to do, Enrique," she says, rather loudly. "This gathering at the last moment. I need to be home, Enrique!" He answers something I cannot understand. The wife decides, "We'll send someone to pick up the girl."

Pausing by the door, I cough, announcing my presence, but they don't interrupt their discussion. He is now saying that he had dismissed the official car for the night. "Maybe—"

"Enrique! We have decided. We'll send someone."

"You were not expecting me today," I say as I enter. "I'm tired, I mean I have been traveling for many hours, some other time . . ."

Yolanda dashes to my side. Placing her arm around my shoulder, she says, "It's just a small group, Camilita. People your age will be there, too. Can you be ready by eight?"

I finally hang my clothes in the armoire, which seems even darker inside, somewhat sinister, like a cave.

I look at my dresses, trying to decide, wishing I could wear something casual to the Lozanos'. I packed a number of dresses, thinking of what my mother often repeated about her country: the meticulous, almost cultivated art of the women to look right on every occasion. I select a pale green dress and white cardigan.

To take a bath, I have to go to the end of the house. The bathroom is not even on the second patio, where the other three bedrooms are, all with closed doors. I find it at last in the small, narrow hall preceding the maids' quarters. Pausing at the door of the bathroom, I peer at the third patio, which is really what is called the *solar*—the backyard: a square of earth with a small garden, mostly roses. Against the wall that encloses the property is the solitary oak that Mama often mentioned.

The bathroom is immense, a snow white room with white tiles covering the floor and the four walls. In the center are four iron chairs around a glass table. Perhaps this unexpected sitting room is what takes away all sense of privacy. The bathtub is very old and uninviting. As I turn on the shower, I understand the purpose of the sitting arrangement: to listen to the concert of the pipes, which sneeze and gurgle and hiccup in high and low notes until at last I receive a violent splash that soon turns into a steady, weak dribble.

"Señorita, you must eat something before you go," Josefa calls as she sees me returning to my room. "Those social dinners are much too late. I have something for you, whenever you're ready."

"I'm starving, Josefa."

A moment later, sitting at the large dining room table by myself, I drink a cup of hot chocolate with white cheese melted in it. Both my father and I used to tease Matesa for this odd combination of melted cheese inside the chocolate until it became a favorite winter treat for the three of us. I'm also eating *arepa con chicharrón* (corn pancakes with bits of pork), another typical dish. Señora Lozano's yellow roses are in the center of the table.

While eating, I look at the portrait. I can't get rid of the discomfort I felt when Lozano showed it to me. Josefa comes into the room. I ask her what she thinks of the picture. "Did you ever meet my grandfather, Josefa?"

"A very distinguished gentleman," she says, with her unalterable expression.

I continue to look at her, waiting to hear something less vague.

"My mother knew him well," Josefa says at last.

"She did? Is your mother still alive?"

"She's very old."

"Josefa!" I burst out. "Can I meet your mother, please? Can I go visit her, Josefa?"

"She's senile, señorita. You probably don't know what that means; you're too young. Very old people like my mother behave like children. They say things they shouldn't say."

"That doesn't matter, Josefa. I just want to ask her a few questions. I wouldn't tire her, I promise. It would be just a short visit, please!"

"In the first place, Señorita Camila, my mother is deaf; one has to shout at her." She keeps her eyes lowered while collecting the empty dishes. "Did you enjoy the *arepa*? Did Señora María Teresa ever make it in your country?"

I limit myself to a nod, disappointed by Josefa's reaction about my visiting the old woman. Maybe Josefa will change her mind.

Back in the room, I get ready. I lie on the bed carefully, trying not to wrinkle my dress, wishing I could go to sleep for the night. The long hours traveling and the excitement of being in San Javier have made me very tired.

"She's like her mother," I hear someone nearby say. Is it Josefa's voice in the next patio?

"God knows what answers my mother will give to the

girl's questions." Josefa is talking to someone. Doesn't she suspect that her voice comes into the room?

I'm half asleep, yet I feel like a wave of hostility is invading the room. "What do you want?" the angry voice of a man asks. "You're like María Teresa, who lived her life asking questions about the past, the past!" I want to answer the angry voice, to say, It's not the past. It's the future that I fear, the regrets I'll carry with me for what I refused to hear, for the moments when I interrupted my mother. I need to learn the answers to the questions I was going to ask someday. I make efforts to speak, but no words come out. Go on, Camila, tell him, a deeper voice within me commands. Again I try to speak, but I'm only mumbling. I hear noises inside the cavelike armoire, as if someone is struggling inside, banging against it.

"Señorita, señorita." Someone is knocking hard on the door. "A señor is here to take you to the fiesta at Señor Lozano's house."

For an instant I don't recognize Pepita's voice; then I realize I'm just waking up from a deep sleep. My heart is still palpitating with fear from my dream. "I'll be out in a minute, Pepita," I answer at last, jumping out of bed.

When I walk out, both Josefa and Pepita are outside. They were worried, they say. "We were both banging at the door. You're dead tired, señorita," Josefa says. They walk with me a few steps along the corridor, Pepita looking at me from head to foot, complimenting my dress, timidly touching my cardigan. "And your hair, señorita, you look *muy linda*."

"When you come back tonight, just press the bell," Josefa instructs.

"Do you have a key, Josefa? I don't want to wake you up."

"Don't let that bother you. I'm awake most of the night taking care of my mother."

"Your mother? I didn't know she was here with you—with us!"

For an instant it looks as if Josefa's mask is going to fall, but the frowning and brief tremor of the lips vanish quickly. Behind her, Pepita has put both hands to her mouth.

"Please ring the bell, señorita," Josefa repeats, walking away to her quarters.

6

A young man with longish hair is framed by the open living room door. "Good evening." He bows, saying nothing else. He stares at me uninhibitedly. After a moment, he says, "I was asked to be here at eight o'clock to drive you to the Lozanos' house."

I find his manner rude. Although he's wearing jeans and an old beige jacket, something about him indicates to me that he's not the family's chauffeur. I don't like the way he has been examining me, as if I were merchandise he's mentally assessing, not quite to his satisfaction.

"Shall we . . . are you ready?" he asks, lifting his arm to look at his watch.

I don't know if I'm ready, I am thinking. I say, "My name is Camila Draper. Who are you?"

Under the corridor lamp, I can see him turning pink.

"Please excuse me. I thought they had told you about me. I am Enrique's brother-in-law, Yolanda's younger brother. My name is Bernardo Arenas."

We walk out. His car is very old, a long black Buick convertible with a funerary look to it. Pronouncing the words slowly, he says in English, "I lament that thees car is not

40

elegant." If I want, he adds in Spanish, we can speak English.

"I prefer to practice my Spanish while I'm here, if you don't mind."

"I also prefer Spanish," he says, opening the door for me yet rushing to his side before I get in. He turns the key, but the engine doesn't respond. I pretend I am busy searching in my purse, although he doesn't seem to be the least uncomfortable as he goes on trying to start the motor. "If you had said you prefer speaking English, I'd have been a mute listener all the way to Enrique's and Yolanda's, although . . . maybe we won't make it," he says, referring to the car as he keeps turning the key in vain. I observe him out of the corner of my eyes. He's not handsome, yet he has an appeal of his own. Perhaps it is his self-confidence, which is almost arrogance. He's not like any of the boys I have known. He's probably in college in one of the nearby cities—Bucaramanga, Zapatoca, Mogotes—spending the July holidays in San Javier. At last, the car begins moving. At the corner parallel to the plaza, a group of men is gathered. "*Hola,* Bernardo, I thought you were gone!"

"Still here," he shouts back, waving.

The plaza is brightly illuminated, the air filled with the music of an old Colombian *cumbia,* a tune I have often heard on one of Matesa's records. A few cars are parked in front of the hotel and to the side of the restaurant. No sooner does the car leave the plaza than it begins ascending a street that turns into a dark hill with no electric posts. I recognize the route, the same the bus took arriving. Bernardo drives with concentration. Weak, sputtering lights appear and disappear momentarily. I imagine candles in the huts along the hill. It's chilly; the wind is stirring my hair. I try closing the window until I discover there's no glass. As we proceed uphill, the road narrows. At one point Bernardo edges the car to the right side of the hill and stops, leaving on his lights. "A car is coming down," he explains. "It looks like a truck, perhaps a bus. Vehicles coming down have the right of way." We wait for what seems a long time. The lights of the approaching vehicle become visible as it rounds the road's many curves. The apprehension I did not feel either flying in the mosquito plane to Bucaramanga or in the bus that brought me to San Javier now weighs heavily on me. I turn to him, hoping he'll say something reassuring, but he's silent, his hand tapping the steering wheel uninterruptedly. Bernardo is as tense as I am. At last we see the lights of a large vehicle advancing cautiously. The heads of two men can be seen in the front seat. "*Gracias. Buenas noches,*" they shout as they pass us. I sigh with relief. At the top of the hill is a building with many lights, perhaps a church. It makes me think of a huge Christmas tree surrounded by darkness. For a while, neither Bernardo nor I speak.

"We are almost there; don't worry. We'll make it," he says at last, moving his hand as if he's going to touch my hand.

Surely he means the car will make it, I think. "The bus driver said the same thing this afternoon, 'We'll make it.' "

"It's a national phrase now, mostly for the benefit of women and children."

42

I turn sharply to look at him. I want to tell him that I have heard about this classification. Mama told me once that when she was in the convent in Bucaramanga, the nuns had a collection of leather-bound books on a shelf in the main hall. One of them was *Don Quijote de la Mancha*. Under the title it read, "Abridged Edition for Women and Children." I say softly, "You mean it's a lie for the foolish and the innocent?"

But he's either not hearing or doesn't care to answer. Something in his rhythm has quickened, perhaps due to his prowess in making it up the hill in his decrepit car.

"See? We're almost there."

I am angry, mostly at the Lozanos. "Why are the Lozanos—" I begin but finish the sentence mentally: exposing me to this.

"We can't stop living," he says, guessing my observation. "That's what the bandits infesting the country would like." He combs his hair with his fingers with quick movements, then, turning toward me, he says, "You must think I am a savage coming to pick you up without introducing myself. Unforgivable."

"You were recovering from your disappointment that I was not a blonde gringa."

He bursts out laughing. "Wrong. I was made speechless by your green-brown eyes . . . and by something else."

"Something else—what?"

"I'll tell you later.

"Later," he repeats when I insist.

"Is that the house?" I point at the lighted building. "It

43

looks like a Christmas tree, or a castle," I say, observing the stone architecture with multiple arches and turrets.

"That's what it is, a castle, 'a useless monster,' as Yolanda calls it when Enrique is not around. A pretentious castle, like the man who built it, Enrique's uncle. He studied architecture in Milano, Italy, where he bought a title, *Conde de Cuchiterra.* He uses a patch on his left eye and wears a black cape that makes him look like—"

"Count Dracula?"

"Rather like a bat. You'll meet him tonight. Be sure to call him *Conde.* To hear it from a pretty girl and in your charming gringo accent will make his night."

"But my Spanish—I don't have an accent, do I?"

He looks at me smiling, not answering. We are now in the stone yard that goes up to the front terrace, where several cars are parked. Bernardo takes something from under his sports jacket and tucks it inside the car's glove compartment. I see that it's a pistol. Stretching his arm to the backseat, he grabs a rolled towel, then gets out of the car and walks around to open the door for me.

"I arrived today and have already seen a number of pistols. Does everyone carry one?"

"Haven't you heard? Well, being a foreigner, you probably don't know the local saying, '*Un hombre sin revolver es un hombre incompleto.*' 'A man without a revolver is half a man.' I personally, like others of my generation, don't give a darn about this stupidity—the old generation's dogma. But the way things are today, carrying a revolver is a necessity. By the way, Camila," he says, holding my arm, "don't be afraid. Enrique and Yolanda will take you back.

44

They were too busy to pick you up. You'll be safer in their car. My pleasure was only one way."

We don't walk up the stone stairs to the front entrance. Instead, Bernardo leads me down a few steps toward a small back door, which leads into a poorly illuminated hall. He explains that we are in the basement. I hear splashing water, voices, and laughter. I realize that what Bernardo is carrying in the rolled towel is his bathing suit. I should have asked, I think, feeling ridiculous in my clothes. "I didn't know it was a pool party," I murmur softly as we come out of the hall, stepping up to the indoor pool, where everyone shouts greetings to Bernardo, asking why he's so late. Only one young woman is not in the pool. She's wearing shorts and an oversized blouse. Putting the towel roll under his arm, he claps, calling for silence. "This is Camila Draper, the guest of honor, the granddaughter of . . . the person whose anniversary, Señor . . . Don—"

"Doctor Pachito Zamora, you idiot," the woman with the oversized shirt corrects while the rest laugh.

I say softly, "He was not a doctor."

The woman outside the pool continues in a loud voice, "And it's not his anniversary, but a thanksgiving tribute. He was a hero, a great man from San Javier."

"He was not a hero," I try to rectify, but no one is listening.

"My name is Patricia," she says as she approaches. Her husband, she explains, is getting refreshments from the bar upstairs. She looks too young to be married. I realize that the oversized blouse is a maternity top. The women swimming on the other side of the pool shout their names: "Clara," "Isabel." The two men with them wave, one saying in unaccented English, "A pleasure to meet you, Camila." Patricia offers me a dish with banana chips, then sits on one of the folding chairs, inviting me to sit on the one next to her.

Bernardo, who had disappeared, is now standing on the springboard, lifting his arms, performing a spectacular dive. Patricia gets up to meet her husband, a very tall man with a moustache who looks twice her age. He's carrying a cigarette between his teeth. His arms are loaded with beer and soda bottles. One of the men in the pool is telling a story that makes the others laugh. Bernardo's interruptions increase the others' laughter. It's clear that they are all close friends, enjoying one another's company. It occurs to me that I, the American girl, am an addition. I feel lonely as well as conspicuous in my inappropriate clothes.

Mrs. Lozano appears. "Here you are. I'm so glad. Bernardo, why didn't you let us know that you had arrived? Really! I was getting worried."

Bernardo and the rest in the pool are unaware of Mrs. Lozano. Yolanda is wearing casual clothes, a colorful skirt and a white, sporty blouse. "Come, Camila, I want to introduce you to the others. They're anxious to meet you. And Enrique has something to tell you. Your uncle called us after we got home today." Turning to the others, Mrs. Lozano shouts, "I imagine you'll prefer having dinner here rather than joining us in the dining room. Am I right?"

Everyone laughs, which apparently means yes, they prefer having dinner by the pool.

"I'm stealing Camila for a while. She'll be back shortly."

No one is listening or noticing that I'm leaving with Mrs. Lozano. The swimmers are still talking, laughing, and splashing. Patricia and her husband are whispering to each other.

"Watch your step, Camila," Yolanda says. "The person who built this place loved stairs." Heavy brass lamps with opaque glass, like the streetlamps in some of Goya's paintings, hang from the ceiling, throwing a creamy light. At the foot of a wide double staircase Yolanda pauses. Turning to me, she says in a confidential tone, "Your uncle was very worried, Camila. Apparently you called this morning early, saying you'd call later to tell them your plans. Learning about the air strike, it occurred to one of your cousins that you might already be in San Javier, and your uncle called Enrique."

"Oh my God, I forgot to call." I put my hands on my face.

"We're all sick with worry these days, Camila. For the first time, I'm grateful that Enrique and I don't have children. But don't worry now. Enrique told them that you were fine and that you couldn't call because the telephone was not yet connected in the house. Wasn't that clever of him? Everything is fine, so let's enjoy ourselves tonight." We begin climbing the stairs. Soft classical music and voices reach me. I am thinking, I didn't feel comfortable with the crowd in the pool; I'll feel less comfortable with the Lozanos' friends. Why did I accept this invitation? The stairs open into a well-lit, impressive salon, where furniture is arranged into three intimate, graceful groups. A piano is in a corner.

47

All the people in the small group turn their heads to look at us as we walk in. The men are together in a corner near the bar: Enrique Lozano; another young man; and two older gentlemen, one with a patch on his eye. Yolanda introduces the two older women on the sofa. One is Margota Alvarez. "You may call me Tita," she tells me and continues knitting. The other one is la señora de Cuchiterra. "And I am Alicia," says a young woman as beautiful as Yolanda. "I have been hearing about you, Camila," she says.

The Count of Cuchiterra bows exaggeratedly as he kisses my hand. All I'm thinking is, He's old enough to remember my grandfather. They are all warm, friendly, complimenting my Spanish, although I have only uttered a brief greeting. The men are wearing ties but no jackets. Everyone is informally dressed. Only la señora de Cuchiterra is wearing a silk dress and cardigan, like me.

"We have been talking about your family," says Lozano. "Victor, his wife, and one of the daughters will be here Friday."

"Tell Camila the other news," Yolanda urges her husband as she passes around a tray with an assortment of cheese and crackers.

"Yes, yes, of course, in a moment," Lozano says, pouring a glass of white wine for me. Returning to his place near the bar, he takes a few sips from his drink, while everyone's eyes are on him, waiting to hear what Yolanda has asked him to say. "Apparently the marble pillar for Don Pachito will only be a first step." He sips from his glass, wipes his mouth slowly with a napkin, and moves closer to the sofa, near the women. "There's a project for a more substantial, permanent tribute."

I feel all eyes on me while I'm trying to decipher Lozano's sentence. At last I ask, "A more permanent . . . that means?"

"That means a bust, for instance," Lozano says.

"Maybe a statue—who knows!" the count adds, accentuating his comment with two steps forward.

"That will show the ladies of the Sociedad Feminista Nacional," says Yolanda. "They have been a nuisance since they heard about Don Pachito's homage, giving Enrique a hard time. Haven't they, dear?"

Lozano nods. "Indeed they have. I wouldn't be surprised if they interrupt Saturday's ceremony with one of their poor taste—"

"Really?" The two ladies on the sofa interrupt in unison. They are all now near the sofa.

"Do you realize, Enriquito," la señora de Cuchiterra continues, raising her voice, "that San Javier is the only town in all this region without a statue, with no monuments, not even a bust, nothing?"

"That was one of my arguments from the beginning when I proposed the memorial for Don Pachito." He turns to me. "I didn't mention it to you this afternoon when I was explaining the difficulties I have encountered, that this feminist organization has been trying for years to have a monument erected to Olympia Hernández."

"Olympia, the teacher?" one of the men asks.

49

"Old Olympia the teacher, yes," answers Lozano, rolling his eyes. "Can you picture San Javier with one single bust or monument erected to . . . a woman?"

I quickly turn to look at Yolanda first, then I search the faces of the other women in the room, who are all nodding, with the exception of the one knitting, who seems to be counting stitches.

I feel my face flushing as I ask, "What's wrong with a woman having a bust or a statue erected in her honor?" In the effort to fight my inhibition, my voice comes out in a falsetto. I look at the other women again, one by one, sure of their support.

"What Enrique means, dear," la señora de Cuchiterra explains, "is that in a town empty of statues or monuments, to have one bust alone dedicated to a woman would be, well, can you imagine?" She turns to look at the others.

"A joke," the count says, closing his eyes, shaking his head.

I don't understand if by "a joke" the count means that he's laughing at public opinion or that he himself believes that to have a bust in San Javier honoring a woman is a mockery.

"A woman is all right, Camila," says Yolanda. "But we must consider the reputation of San Javier. If at last, after all his efforts, Enrique obtained authorization and funds to have the first pillar dedicated to a native son, let it be for a man like your grandfather, who did much to improve the town."

50

"Of course." "*Sí.*" "Indeed." "*Absolutamente.*" Everyone agrees with Yolanda.

"It's my turn," Tita, on the sofa, says, causing the others to laugh. She folds her knitting, setting it away. "A woman is just as entitled to be honored and recognized for her merits as a man. I'm not saying"—she turns to me—"that I don't agree that your grandfather deserves this honor. He does, of course. But so does this woman Olympia Hernández. She dedicated her whole life to teaching the children of San Javier to read and write. Let me finish." She raises a hand toward the men, who begin segregating themselves again near the bar.

Half smiling, Lozano and the other men return, giving their attention to Tita. "Olympia turned her house into a school. She herself was a humble woman with little education, yet with an ardent ideal. She sold eggs from her little farm at the market every Saturday."

"And paper flowers that she made at night," Tita's husband adds.

"To get money for books and benches and all the utensils she needed for her pupils," Tita continues.

"Commendable . . . commendable indeed," the count interrupts. "And how, my dear Tita, do you happen to know all this?"

"In the first place, everyone who was born in San Javier knows it. Then a pamphlet was distributed not long ago. Why, Count, you must have received one yourself. Maybe you didn't care to read it. The Sociedad Feminista put it out. It had a brief biography of Doña Olympia."

"Was my grandfather alive when this woman was teaching?"

"As a matter of fact, Camila, your grandfather is mentioned in this pamphlet repeatedly," says Tita.

"He was one of her first pupils," Tita's husband cuts in. "Your grandfather walked miles to come from his parents' farm. He was not rich then, just a poor boy really. It was later, as I'm sure you've been told, that he acquired his famous horses."

"In accordance with this biography," Tita says, "it was Doña Olympia who inspired Francisco Zamora years later to donate a house, the first school of San Javier—"

"Escuela Olympia Hernández," Tita's husband completes his wife's sentence. "Your grandfather called it that in her honor."

Everyone is silent. I am envisioning a boy walking through plains and hills, panting, arriving for his daily classes . . . Doña Olympia welcoming him, giving my grandfather the treasure of words. I am not sure if it's the boy or the woman who moves me more. "What a beautiful story," I murmur.

The others look at me, smiling.

"We'll get you the little biography. You'll like to have it," Tita and her husband promise in unison.

I am glad I am here tonight, glad to meet Tita and her husband. I like her soft yet determined manner as she spoke of Olympia Hernández. Tita's character makes me think of my mother.

I turn to the count, who has been smiling. "I'm anxious to meet someone who remembers my grandfather and was his friend. Did you know him, Count? Were you his friend?"

The count's smile turns into a frown. I feel embarrassed, realizing he's unflattered that I'm identifying him as the oldest in the group.

"I spent many years in Europe," he answers at last. "As I was telling Enrique a moment ago, I often feel like a foreigner in this place."

"It's just that I'm eager to hear some anecdote, something that will bring him to life for me," I add as an apology.

There's silence in the room. Again I feel all eyes on me. I perceive their warmth and something else that turns the room somber. Is it pity because I lost my mother, I wonder, or does it have to do with my grandfather being remembered for "that thing," as Lozano said.

Tita breaks the silence. "You learned something about him tonight. Why bother to ask others, Camila? Some things . . . just let them be. Enjoy yourself while you're here; be proud of your grandfather."

I can't help noticing the quick glance that la señora de Cuchiterra and Yolanda exchange.

"I took you away from the others, Camila," Yolanda says. "You have had enough of us, the *older* group." She begins leaving the room, explaining that it is time to check on dinner. Alicia gets up, following her to the kitchen. The men have returned to their corner. At the door Yolanda calls, "You know your way to the pool, Camila?"

"Yes, I know," I answer, but I walk toward the window, which is really a balcony enclosed by glass. From there I see the hill with the huts' twinkling candles and at the bottom the alternating darkness and lights of San Javier's panorama.

"Camila." Someone is calling me. I quickly turn my head and see Bernardo across the room near the stairway. He seems unwilling to enter the room. He's making a gesture for me to come with him. His wet hair looks longer. For some reason of my own that I don't bother to analyze, I ignore Bernardo. Turning my back, I remain on the balcony.

"Camila." His voice, now louder, attracts the attention of the two ladies on the sofa and the count, who has joined them. The count calls, "Come in, come in. When are you going to cut that mane of yours? Long hair is for girls." He bursts out laughing at his own joke.

"Come join us, Bernardito," la señora de Cuchiterra calls.

Realizing that Bernardo has been trying to avoid the others in the room, maybe the count in particular, I walk toward him.

~8 7 8~

Everyone in the pool is now dressed, the girls in jeans and sporty blouses, the men as casually as Bernardo. There are candles on the table, which is covered with trays of roasted chicken laced with fresh pineapple, rice with black olives, small tamales, fruit salad, and a fountain with *arequipe,* a dessert made of milk and sugar. Yolanda is lighting the big candle at the center of the table. Shaking the match, she says, "Enjoy it!"

"*Gracias,* Yolanda!" they all chorus.

The young women begin serving plates to their partners first, then they help themselves. Attention, however, is concentrated on a corner of the pool, where the husband of the young girl is bending over something I cannot see properly. It's dark; the only light is provided by the candles. Patricia, near her husband, is also stooped over. One moment, she's holding a lantern so her husband can see; the next, she's feeding him with morsels from her plate.

"*¿Qué pasa?*" Bernardo shouts. "You need help, Carlos?"

"It's coming!" Carlos answers. Perhaps a dish is being cooked at the last moment, I imagine, but it must be something more important. There's a tension, a kind of seriousness, as when one is about to participate in a solemn ceremony.

The camaraderie displayed in the pool has disappeared. Now they are all silent, simultaneously eating and looking up toward the corner at the couple.

"It's coming. Get ready!" both husband and wife shout. "The fiesta has begun!" Loud music pours from their corner. Is this, dancing music, the cause of all the expectancy? I wonder, turning to Bernardo. He puts his half-empty plate on the edge of the table, moving his head and shoulders to the rhythm of a Colombian *porro*, his face intensely serious. The beating sound grows louder, intrusive. I have a chicken wing in my hand, which I'm enjoying. Bernardo whisks it away, wiping my fingers with a napkin, pulling me up from the chair. They are all dancing now on the terrace behind the diving board. I am somehow resisting the music, refusing to be seduced like the others, as if I am the carrier of a mission I have come to accomplish in San Javier that excludes this triviality, as if I should remain an outsider, a stranger in this ceremony of jerks and contortions surrounding me. Bernardo presses me against him one moment, the next he throws me away, holding my arm, twirling me again and again. "Loosen up, loosen up," I hear the voice of the drums commanding; *"¡Menéate, muchacha!"* the flutes scream. I look around at the girls. Like Bernardo, they are all absorbed in their solos, eyes closed, faces with the fervor of praying. I am now intent on emulating Bernardo's jerks forward and backward, his half-grotesque yet graceful jumps, which harmonize with the music. At last, as if caught by surprise, I find myself also immersed in the dance, my solo, so deft in my performance, I am not only inventing my own jerks and contortions but stealing Bernardo's improvisations. We look at each other, our heads nodding incessantly to the tempo of a *merecumbé.* For the first time in months, I am not feeling pain or remorse, nor am I haunted by the memory of the silences I imposed on my mother. Tonight I'm free of the tumult of questions I want to ask that I cannot formulate to myself, either in English or Spanish. I know only that the questions are there, within me, weighty as rocks.

We are dancing now, a slow number. He puts my head against his shoulder. Closing my eyes, I mutter, *"Gracias."*

"You're welcome," he says, pulling away to look at me. "Why are you laughing?"

"I'm grateful for the pleasurable evening, the dancing."

"Friday night is dancing night at the club. Would you come with me? We'll dance until—"

"My uncle and his family will be here. I'll be with them."

"What about tomorrow? After I leave work, we could—"

"Tomorrow I have plans."

"I'd like to see you again, Camila. Maybe you'll finish early."

"I prefer not to make any plans. I don't know at what time—"

"All right. Thursday—reserve that evening for me, *¿sí?*"

"Yes," I say while I'm thinking of my visit to the priest tomorrow morning. "Pachito who?" many asked. I am remembering Lozano's words. ". . . But they all remember him for the other thing, ah, yes, for *that* their memory of Francisco Zamora remains clear." How is it possible, I reproach myself, that the words of a stranger can so easily turn me disloyal to the memory of my grandfather?

"*Tranquila,* Camila," Bernardo whispers near my ear, perhaps sensing my tension. "Take it eesy," he adds. "Is that how you say it in English?"

"I prefer '*Tranquila,* Camila,'" I say.

Through the window I see daylight. In a moment the church bells will be calling for Mass, which I'll attend before speaking to the priest. I turn to look at my wristwatch on the night table. It's then I realize that it is past midday. "Oh no!" I shout, sitting up. The Lozanos brought me home at dawn. When Josefa opened the door, she said, "You need a good rest. I left a thermos with chamomile tea in your room." Now, looking at the thermos, I can't reject the thought that Josefa put something in the tea to keep me sleeping. I never heard the church bells, nor was I conscious of anything around me. The house is silent. I feel as if there's a conspiracy to stop me from seeing San Javier and learning about my grandfather. Quickly, I get out of bed and put on my robe. "Another day wasted," I hear myself mumbling. Uncle Victor and his family will be here soon, and my plans will be interrupted. Such is the silence of the house, I'm tempted to call Josefa or Pepita, yet I find myself tiptoeing my way to the bathroom, trying not to be noticed, beginning to recognize my intentions.

After my bath, I dress in a rush, saying to myself that I have an excuse—I can explain that I was looking for Josefa or Pepita. As I step into the maids' quarters, I hear some-one singing softly, then voices coming from the side where the backyard is. I can see Josefa kneeling on the ground. Pepita is handing her something, perhaps a garden tool. They seem to be planting a bush beside the roses.

I hesitate in the narrow corridor where there's an old, broken rocking chair between two doors. Farther, closer to the backyard, is a third door, which is probably the maids' bathroom. I knock softly on the first door. "May I?" I wait, then push open the door, seeing immediately that it's Pepita's room. On the wall, at the head of her bed, are glossy pictures of American movie actors and others I don't recognize, perhaps local celebrities. The glossy pictures are arranged around a colorful framed image of the Sacred Heart of Jesus. Thrown over the unmade bed is a plastic bag with the ribbons Pepita wears on her ponytail. On a low table with a mirror attached to it are several jars, mostly of nail polish. A soiled rag doll leans against the mirror. One wall is covered with Pepita's clothes, her dresses on wire hangers hanging from nails. Although there's only the narrow bed and the table with the mirror, the space is so stingy, I wonder how Pepita moves about. I close her door and turn to the second door. The low singing I have been hearing comes from inside, either from a TV or a radio. "May I come in?" I call. No one an-swers, but I know Josefa's mother is inside. At last I push open the door softly. My heartbeat accelerates as I see an old woman on a chair between two narrow beds. Head bent to one side, mouth half open, the woman is sleeping. She stirs slightly, perhaps sensing my presence or the light through the door, which I left ajar. I approach cautiously. I pause near the radio, which rests on a wooden box covered with an old towel. I kneel in front of the woman, placing my hand softly on the blanket protecting her legs. They feel fleshless, the bones protruding like stones. *"Hola,"* I whisper, struggling between staying and leaving. The old woman half opens her eyes; her face gradually acquires an expression of wonder. Then in the eyes, fully open, I detect a light of recognition. *"¡Mi niña Tesita . . . Tesita!"* she begins, her hands pushing forward to my face, groping in the air, touching my cheeks, my nose. "My child, *mi niñaaaa.*" She's now wailing.

"Shhhh, don't be afraid, I'm Camila, María Teresa's daughter. I came to—" I interrupt myself as the woman's crying turns louder. I wrap her hands gently in mine.

"They took her away—"

"Who? Who was taken away? Tell me," I ask, "tell me."

"I promised her I'd look after you, my Tesita." She begins kissing my hands, wetting them with tears and saliva.

"They keep me locked in this room. That man"—she screams something else I can't understand, then—"he's burning in hell."

"Shhhh." I press the woman's head against me. "Don't cry. I'm here with you, please don't cry." I go on for a moment, patting her head, eager to pacify her.

Light invades the room abruptly. I turn. Josefa, inside the room, has switched on the ceiling bulb. Next to her is Pepita, her eyes popping out of their sockets. "What are you doing here? You're trespassing. This is not done here!" Josefa yells.

61

"I'm sorry, I just . . . I didn't hear you and came to find . . ." I mumble, putting my hands to my face, which feels flushed and hot. I move away from the old woman, who throws her arms toward me, crying, mumbling unintelligibly. She seems aware only of me in the room.

"What right do you have to disturb an old woman?" Josefa shouts as she pushes down her mother's arms, asking Pepita to get her a cup of the herb water from the aluminum pitcher in the kitchen. Pepita dashes out, returning immediately with a cup. She and Josefa bend over the old woman. In the agitation, the blanket has fallen, exposing the fleshless legs, which are like toothpicks.

"I didn't mean—I'm so sorry," I keep mumbling.

Leaving her mother, Josefa walks toward me near the door. "We're poor and humble, but we keep our place. You should keep yours, too. Please leave us alone!" She pushes me with one hand; with the other she closes the door.

Although Josefa's touch is soft, her trembling, her whole attitude, show an anger I have not caused in anyone before. Hands on my face, I walk back to my room feeling ashamed, repentant, and confused. I sit on the bed. More than anything, I am shaken by a suspicion that is absurd, yet I feel it growing within me. I recall Mama saying one day that many families in San Javier had a sister or a brother or some other relative locked in a back room of the house, either because she or he was insane or had some physical deformity. "They keep me locked in this room," she complained to me. Could the lady in Josefa's room . . . could she be my grandmother? The more I repeat the question, the more I realize the absurdity of my supposition. I look at the walls, as if the pictures there could console me. If only Mama were here to answer my questions. I begin sobbing. It's dark in the room. I don't bother to turn on the lamps. I can hear the faraway voices of Josefa and Pepita and also the faint lamentation of the old woman, sad, piercing, like a flute.

I go to the basin in the closet, turning on the light. I wash my face, looking away from the reflection of my red eyes in the mirror. As I step out into the room, I hear steps approaching.

"Señorita," Josefa calls, her voice now without anger. "May I come in? I want to apologize—to explain." She walks in and turns on the lamp by the rocking chair. "I had no right—it's not my place to speak to you like that. Please accept my apologies, señorita."

I point at the thermos on my night table with an accusing finger. "You put something in the tea to keep me sleeping . . . away from her."

Josefa shakes her head, smiling sadly. "I gave you chamomile tea to relax you. From the first moment I sensed your—I don't know the word—restlessness, anguish? In every garden in this town people cultivate herbs— *manzanilla, hierbabuena.* We've used them since the time of Adam and Eve for nerves, indigestion, colds, everything. Surely, Señorita Camila, you don't believe me capable of putting anything—"

My eyes dart to the portrait of my grandmother. Josefa turns to look at the picture also, then at me, frowning.

"Is that woman in your room really your mother?" I ask,

looking at Josefa intently. "She thought I was my mother and was calling me 'my Tesita.' Tell me the truth."

"The truth? What do you mean, señorita? Of course she's my mother. Who did you think—Oh my God!" Josefa finally understands. She goes on shaking her head slowly. "Señorita, I worry about you. How can you believe . . ." She moves closer. "May I?" she asks, sitting on the bed by my side. "How can you believe that Doctor Victor, who adored his mother, would allow her to be living with me, a maid, in that dark, miserable room that he himself calls a hole? Doña Adelaida is dead. She died long ago. Surely you know that, señorita?"

I don't answer. I feel sorrow coming from the woman, puzzlement also. I know she's telling me the truth. Perhaps to justify my ridiculous supposition, I ask, "Why then was she throwing her arms at me?"

"She thought you were Señora María Teresa. That's why she was calling you 'mi niña Tesita.' " While Josefa talks, she rubs my back softly. "Mama was Señora María Teresa's nanny. She loved your mother. Sometimes my mother would travel with your mother to Bucaramanga, to the places Don Pachito was always sending the children. Then, when your mother was sent away to Bucaramanga for the last time, Mama never recovered from losing her. Señora María Teresa must have told you that she spent her teen years at the house of her aunt Chinca, Don Francisco's sister, in Bucaramanga."

"I know," I say. My mother had told me about her aunt Chinca, who had married a man twice her age and had been left a widow. I am ashamed of my childish behavior. "I'm sorry, Josefa, I've upset you."

"What can I do to help you? What would make you happy, señorita?"

"Would you answer my questions?"

Josefa doesn't respond for a moment. Then she says, "Don't you think that your uncle is the one to tell you all you want to know?" She lifts my chin with her hand, looks into my eyes, then smiles. "I'm only a maid watching over this house. By the way, Señorita Camila, a moment ago, while I was in the garden, I was commenting to Pepita that you haven't seen your grandfather's rooms upstairs. I'll get your dinner, then you'll go up and see them, ¿sí?"

"I want to, very much. Would you come with me, Josefa?"

"You go by yourself. You'll feel close to him there." She points at the ceiling. "That was his private world."

An unobtrusive door in one corner of the dining room opens to the staircase that leads to the second floor. The door has a small bell attached to the back, which rings every time the door opens. The bell, Josefa explained a moment ago, was to call my grandfather for lunch and dinner. "You see, at the end, after he got rid of the horses and the farm, when it was only he and Señora Chinca in the house, Don Pachito spent all his time up there—alone."

"Didn't he sleep in the room I'm staying in?"

"Sometimes, but his world was up there. Ring the bell when you're ready to come down." She takes a long, rusty key from one of the drawers of the sideboard. "I always keep the door closed."

Now, ascending the dark, creaking stairway, I feel fear. The darkness increases as I go on climbing. I pause, wondering if I shouldn't come down and tell Josefa that I'd rather see Grandfather's room in the daylight. I feel a heaviness in front of me, as if someone is waiting for me at the end of the stairs—the ghost of my grandfather? But his ghost would not give me this palpitation I'm feeling. Is it what I might find . . . the truths I didn't hear from Matesa? I ask myself. As I finally reach the top of the stairs, I see that the foyer is illuminated by a ceiling lamp. It's a spacious foyer furnished with a red leather sofa and three armchairs. A painting, facing the stairs, shows hunters and their dogs returning home with pheasants and ducks. In the background, two men are carrying a bleeding deer between themselves. Close to the sofa is a cupboard with glasses, unfinished bottles of Rum Santander, and cognac. A strong aroma of coffee seems to exude from every corner. I stand there, aware that my initial fright has turned into exhilaration, a feeling of reverence. I tiptoe about as if I'm entering a sacred place—my grandfather's world!

To the left, the foyer narrows into a hall with a door that opens to a salon as big as a gymnasium, taking the whole space of the second floor. A piece of furniture I have never seen before attracts my attention. It resembles the peaked roof of a house, with several shelves where revolvers are encased behind a glass door. In the top compartment are pistols in white turtle shell, others in silver, a tiny one in gold, a variety of weapons that would probably intrigue a collector or an expert but that leave me indifferent. The rifles and bayonets are in the lower compartments. An old, scratched desk, which is actually a table with a chair, the only chair in the huge room, sits against the wall. It seems strange to me that, while the walls are cluttered with hanging whips, reins, a variety of stirrups, two immense leather cowboy hats, even a pair of black and white sheepskin riding chaps, the room is empty of furniture, except for the desk and chair, the arms cabinet, and a couch with an armrest at one end. Two paintings of horses are also on the wall. One resembles a picture I have seen in Papa's book of Remington's sculptures: a horse standing on its rear legs, the rider holding the reins in one hand, waving his hat with the other. Head and arm raised, the rider seems to be saluting the sky. The other painting shows a column of wild horses galloping on a field, manes and tails flying in the wind. The only photographs in the room are on the wall above the desk, a repeated picture of the same black horse. Colibrí? Relámpago? I wonder, knowing that Caracol was a white horse. There's no selectivity or taste in the display of these equestrian objects, as if the intention was simply to find a place for them. Lying on the floor against the wall are English and Western saddles.

I approach the desk, which looks disorderly ordered. Folders and papers are piled at either side; a stained silver horseshoe rests on one of the stacks. I take a folder and leaf through it. A cloud of dust comes out. I continue searching through the papers, which are mostly invoices and a few business letters dating from the fifties and early sixties. Some pages have been burned at the edges by a cigarette. I look in vain for something personal. I know Mama collected her own letters to her father when she came to San Javier at the time of his death. "Papa preserved every one of Victor's and my letters," she told me. One faded yellow program of a horse exhibition is the most personal of the papers. At the top of the program, the name *Francisco Zamora* is printed in large letters. I keep looking at Grandfather's name, eager to feel some emotion. The papers exude a vague smell of tobacco.

I move to the end of the room to investigate the two doors. One leads to a small bathroom. The other door opens to a closet filled with riding boots; some have stirrups still strapped to them. To one side of the closet, attached to the wood of the top shelf, is a small picture of a boy with a perplexed expression that mirrors my own mood. I recognize Uncle Victor by his cleft chin. He was probably eight or nine at the time the picture was taken. The closet's top shelf seems empty. I have the impression that everything has been left untouched, even the dust. I stand here, disappointed in this "private world" of my grandfather where nothing makes me feel his presence. As I move away to close the door, I see something at the back of the top shelf. It's a bulky object wrapped in a brown blanket. I stand on my toes and manage to pull the blanket, bringing it down. I set it on the couch. As I begin unwrapping the package, I can feel the pear-shaped body of a mandolin. My hands move faster. Then at last I see the instrument, which has one single string. Lovingly I hug the mandolin. Attached to it with a piece of Scotch tape is an ivory plectrum. Was this perhaps his favorite mandolin among the many he had? I wonder, caressing the soft wood. After a moment, I place it carefully on the couch and continue unfolding the blanket until I find a large red and green wooden spinning top. The letter *V* had been scratched on it with a nail or some pointed object. The last thing inside the blanket is an old-fashioned porcelain doll with brown glass eyes that keep fluttering, opening and closing as I turn it in my hands. I press the doll against my bosom, closing my eyes and imagining my mother as a little girl, playing with it. The musical instrument and the toys seem to be impregnated with a melancholy that reaches to me. Grandfather's mandolin with the single string resembles a human face with the mouth open in a scream, showing a tooth. Did Grandfather himself place these things together as a symbol of what he loved most in his life—his children and his musical instrument? What about his wife? "Why was Grandmother excluded?" No sooner do I whisper the words than I hear a knock from inside the closet. I have a sudden impulse to run. What could it be? I wonder. A rat, a mouse? After a moment, I move near the closet. From the door, standing on my toes, I see a brown object, like a block, which I had not noticed when I pulled down the package with the mandolin and the toys. In the middle of the shelf, the square thing is unreachable. I rush to bring the chair from the desk and step on it. The object is a leather box. It had probably been pushed upward against the wall by the large package and fell down, making the noise. I stand still. Has anyone else seen it besides Grandfather? It's clear that he wanted to hide it, making it invisible behind the mandolin and the toys. The box probably contains Grandmother's jewelry. Finally I reach for it. The leather box is engraved with primitive Indian masks and is lightweight. I feel excitement mixed with tension, as I imagine it might contain something more interesting than jewels. Some family revelation, a secret? I'm immobile on the chair, holding the box. A duel between curiosity and fear is taking place within me. As I carefully step down, I know that curiosity is the winner. I sit on the chair inside the closet, the box in my lap. My eyes are fixed on the golden closing bar, a familiar mechanism. Should I slide it, find out? My hands don't move. I give a start as I hear a bell ringing.

"Are you ready to come down, Señorita Camila?" Josefa's voice interrupts my reflections. "I found an old lantern to light the stairs," she calls.

Anxious to find a place where I can conceal the box, I push it under the elastic of my underwear. I look pregnant. My skirt pocket is too small. It's not until I hear Josefa's steps coming up that I place the box on the floor in a corner, then rush to pick up the blanket with the mandolin and toys, pushing everything into the closet, turning off the closet's light, closing the door.

"I'm coming, Josefa," I answer at last. I'll be back, I promise myself. I'll sneak up to rescue the leather box and find out what it contains.

❧10❧

The street is quiet; the only sound is that of the church bells calling to Mass and of my low-heel pumps striking on the pavement. At the corner, entering the plaza, a man with a horse cart is selling tomatoes, guavas, oranges, and other produce. A collar of gardenias and red and pink hibiscus adorns the horse's neck. The animal's head appears to be floating in a sea of flowers.

The steps up to the church terrace don't have enough space for my feet. They were built long ago for tiny people with tiny feet. I try to climb sideways.

The church is half empty. A few peasant women, some wearing straw hats, others shawls, occupy the pews closest to the entrance. The townspeople are scattered in the other pews.

Mass is already in progress. I can't follow the Spanish of either the priest or the parishioners until I finally understand that the Mass is being said in Latin.

In this church my grandfather and my mother and uncle were baptized. Were my grandparents married here also? I know that Grandmother came from another state.

I notice that most of the statues of saints are dark,

monklike figures. The only light colors are the blue and pink in the statues of the Virgin and Holy Child. The columns and walls are covered with soot. I look at the main altar's background. I'm curious, eager to see the image of God emerging from the tempestuous sky that frightened my mother as a child, but the wall is covered with heavy blue drapes. Is the painting still there? I wonder. Has it been covered because it also frightened other children? Maybe the priest will allow me to take a peek at it after I speak with him. A painting of the Purgatory fills the arched roof. It shows women submerged in fire, their long hair mingling with the flames. Curiously, no men are shown in this illustration of suffering sinners. Is there a message here for the women and children of San Javier—that men die and go straight to heaven? Above the burning victims, the crowned Virgin sits on a cloud, a benign smile on her lips as she surveys the sinners in the pool of flames. Ahead of me I see several cushioned pews with names of the owners on small plaques.

There's something grandiose about the church, yet deterioration shows in several places. In the pulpit the carved head of one of the apostles is missing its nose. The wood of some of the pews is also cracked and unfinished.

A man is singing in a nasal, quivering voice, "Have pity on me, my Lord, have pity on me." A dog lying comfortably in the aisle, head inclined to one side, seems entranced by the cantor.

The priest shuffles about with difficulty, dragging his feet as he walks from one end of the altar to the other. I hear the handbell ringing—the altar boy calling for Communion. When my turn comes, the priest stops. With the host in his hand, he stands there, shaking his head disapprovingly. At last, I understand. He will not place the Communion in my palm. I stick out my tongue. I'm annoyed for calling attention to myself. Will the pastor be predisposed against me? I'm thinking as I return to my pew.

At the end of the Mass, I wait for everyone to leave. I follow a stout lady with a white mantilla, who is following a middle-aged couple and a campesina who is holding the hand of a little boy. We enter the room adjacent to the sacristy.

"Señora." I touch the shoulder of the lady with the mantilla. "I didn't make an appointment with the padre; perhaps I should—"

"Not at all," she says, waving a hand. "It's not the custom here; one comes when one needs to come."

"You're in the wrong place!" protests a skinny old man wearing a dark, shrunken suit. "This way, this way!" he calls. We step out into a brick corridor, where we stand in line near the first door.

The man now orders us to move backward, farther from the door. He throws both hands at us as if we are chickens or pigs he's scaring away. "You go first." He points at me, the last in line.

"I'll wait for my turn," I say.

Moving closer to me, he insists. "Go in, *por favor.*" Then to the others he explains, "The foreign girl first."

The lady with the mantilla encourages me to go in. "I'm just here to have my new rosary blessed," she explains, displaying a beautiful gold rosary with emerald beads between the decades.

I smile at the others apologetically as I enter the dark room. Quickly they all move closer to the door, as if a show is about to start. I look at the door, wishing to close it. A large, dusty stone is placed on the floor to keep it open. A chair is in front of a messy desk. The priest, now in his black soutane, is in a corner, bending over a long table with large books, perhaps missals.

"*Buenos días,* Padre—" His name escapes me at that moment.

He doesn't answer. I pause near the chair, waiting for him to take his seat behind the desk, but he doesn't seem aware of anyone around him. There's something frantic in the priest's movements as he goes from one corner of the table to the other, giving order to the books, separating them from the stacks of paper. One moment he sets a book in one place, the next he removes it, holding it in his hands, hesitating, shaking his head. He, who moved sluggishly celebrating Mass, seems now possessed by an urgency, as if he had been told he has one hour to give order to the messy room. Turning at last, he makes a gesture for me to speak.

I introduce myself, then say, "Padre, I arrived the day before yesterday to attend the homage for my grandfather, Francisco Zamora, this weekend."

Moving his hands up and down, he urges me to speak faster.

"Padre—Padre Roque." I'm delighted to remember his name. "I come from the United States—you knew my grandfather, Francisco Zamora, Don Pachito, that's how he was called here. I'd be so happy, Padre, if you would tell me something you remember about him." While talking, I'm thinking. How absurd to be here with the others, instead of making an appointment for later on in the day and talking to him privately.

He approaches his desk at last and sits in the chair, putting a hand to his ear. He says, "Again." I recall instantly the boy Tomás carrying my suitcase, telling me, "Padre Roque is as deaf as a wall."

"Padre Roque," I begin anew, repeating what I had said.

A murmur of approval at my raising my voice comes from the others waiting by the door.

The priest bows, covering his face with both hands. He's trying to recall something, I say to myself, feeling expectant. Several minutes elapse. The room grows silent. Although I have moved my chair so that my back is to the door, I can see that the campesina's little boy has installed himself inside the room. He's now sitting on the stone by the door. I turn; the others, all staring, seem intrigued by the priest's silence. Has he gone to sleep? I wonder in consternation.

"United States," he shouts, as if these two words alone make sense to him. "A saintly woman."

"Who, Padre—my mother?"

He shakes his head.

"My grandmother? Do you remember her?"

"*Claro!* Of course!" he shouts even louder. "No one in San Javier has forgotten Doña Adelaida, no one!"

My heart accelerates. Why is my grandmother so remembered by everyone? I wonder, but my question is, "And my grandfather, Padre. Do you also remember him?"

Someone in the audience by the door clears his throat.

The padre doesn't answer. Head bent, his clasped hands are resting on the desk. "Her singing—I still hear her songs while I say Mass." Lifting one hand, he shakes it for a moment. "Enough!" he says softly, as if he's speaking to himself. "There are remorses clinging to the soul like bloodsuckers." He shakes his head. "Remorses one carries to the tomb."

My heart gives a jump. What is he talking about? Whose remorses? Is he talking about himself? My grandparents? I'm overcome by anguish. "Padre, would you prefer if I come back?" I ask after a moment. "What time would be convenient?"

"Have mercy on me. Too many sinners, too many memories. Your grandfather, *he*,"—the priest makes a peculiar sound with his throat, then slowly, between his teeth, biting the letters, says—"F r a n c i s c o Z a m o r a."

"Francisco Zamora," I repeat, as if my grandfather's name is a prayer that would pacify my sudden alarm and confusion. I'm aware that the others waiting for their turn are now all inside the room. I wonder if it's the lady with the rosary who sighs so deep a sigh I feel it on my neck like wind blowing into the room.

"Go on," the padre orders.

I'm embarrassed. Once more I have to go through the whole description of myself and my grandfather and the memorial. "I came to attend—"

"Speak louder!" a man shouts from somewhere outside the room. "Louder!"

With closed eyes, I yell my little speech about my grandfather and the weekend ceremony, begging the priest at the end to tell me what he recalls about my grandparents. I can feel myself blushing, but this time I'm sure he heard me.

He opens one of the desk drawers and begins fumbling.

I sigh with relief: He's probably looking for a photograph, a letter he preserved from my grandfather, some memento. His face has turned friendly.

"Did you notice the church?"

"Yes, Padre, very pretty. My mother told me it's a very old church." I am now shouting uninhibitedly.

"Very old, like me," he says, laughing, continuing his search. The others inside the room are also laughing.

"I'm beyond repair," he adds. I join the others, whose laughter increases. I turn my head toward them. They look at me, laughing, nodding, agreeing, that in spite of his old age and deafness, Padre Roque has not lost his sense of humor.

At last Padre Roque brings out a dirty file, extracting from it a yellowish document, which he unfolds and displays over his messy desk.

With discouragement I read the big letters, *Iglesia del Rosario, San Javier.* It's a drawing for renovation of the church.

He makes a sign for me to approach. "See? There's much that can be done to restore the nobility of our church. See?" he repeats, his bony hands showing me places on the plan. He mumbles about the confessional boxes, the pulpit, the broken statues. "You understand, I'm sure. You have beautiful churches in the United States."

I look away, anger and frustration dominating me. Still I manage to say, "Maybe someone among your parishioners, you know, someone who still remembers . . . an old farmer, a campesino?"

He puts a hand on his forehead. "My child, there's no such thing as an old campesino. They die young. If a campesino reaches fifty, he's ancient." In silence he goes on looking at the map. His freckled, bony hands are two crawling spiders pointing here and there. "No one cares anymore for the Casa de Dios. They make parks, tall buildings, roads, homages . . . h o m a g e s," he repeats slowly, closing his eyes. "Even the campesinos don't throw their coins as they used to." Reluctantly, he begins folding the drawing, inserting it back into the dirty folder. He's silent for a moment. Then, in a soft, humble tone, he says, "Anything helps."

I can sense now the restlessness of the others waiting their turn. The campesina's boy is whimpering softly. It's clear that the priest will tell me nothing, whether he remembers my grandparents or not. He's looking at me, waiting.

I open my purse. I don't have enough Colombian pesos, but I do have a twenty-dollar bill and two tens. I take one of the ten-dollar bills, then, as I'm about to set it on the desk, I quickly grab the twenty-dollar bill and give it to him.

"God bless you." His smile is a dark knot of wrinkles. We stand up simultaneously, he mumbling a few words in Latin, blessing me, then offering his hand for me to kiss.

I take the papery hand and begin bending but not enough to kiss it.

"I'm sorry it took so long," I murmur to the others, who are all looking at me pityingly. The campesina puts a hand on her face, twisting her head to one side. The couple says in unison, "Maybe *mañana* you'll have luck, señorita." The señora with the mantilla mutters, "He's half gone, you know, dear."

I walk back into the church to leave. There's no one around. Without lights, the church is very dark. I pause midway in the aisle, realizing that my face is wet, that without my being aware of it, my frustration is pouring out in tears I cannot contain. I fumble for a Kleenex.

"Señorita . . . señorita," a man's voice calls. "I know someone who knew your grandfather."

I cannot see who's saying it. The voice comes from the side of the altar. "Who? Can you tell me? Where are you?"

From the darkness of the nave a shadow advances. It's the skinny man in the shrunken suit who had asked me, "the foreign girl," to go ahead of the others. "How long are you staying in town?"

"I'll be leaving after the weekend ceremony. Would you please tell me the name—whatever you have to say?" I am upset with myself for thinking, This man wants to collect something from me.

"Don Teodoro Espinoza, that's his name. He was Don Francisco Zamora's friend until the end."

80

"Until the end?" I murmur, more to myself.

"Don Teodoro lives down by the river with his daughter, an old maid. Don't tell anyone I told you about him, least of all don't tell Doctor Victor, your uncle." He moves his hands back and forth. "It's really not my place to—"

"Never mind. Down by the river, you said. Did you know my grandfather?"

"I didn't know anyone in your family." He takes a step backward, putting both hands in front of his face as if my questions are stones he wants to protect himself from. "I have been in this town only a few years, but one hears rumors. This place is good for that. I'm an outsider; I come from Zapatoca, where I was the sacristan for many years until a new priest came and replaced me with a younger man." His mouth is half open; for a moment he resembles a child about to cry.

"Why didn't the priest tell me anything? He remembers my grandmother. He said she was a saint."

"Bahh!" The sacristan slaps the air. "Padre Roque says that about everyone who's dead. It's the ones who are alive he can't bear."

"Is there a bus I can take to go see Don Teodoro?"

"No buses in this town. It's far, but not that far for a young person like you to walk. The Espinozas live in a red house; Las Piedras, that's the name of Don Teodoro's place. Be patient; he's not as bad as Padre Roque, but he's also deaf."

"Deaf? Come on," I mumble, wondering if this is some joke. Josefa's mother, the priest, and now Don Teodoro.

"Is everyone who can tell me something about my grandfather deaf? I can't believe it!"

"Old age, señorita. Don't people get old in the United States?"

"Are you willing to go with me, please?" Sliding my purse from my shoulder, I begin to open it.

Immediately the man moves backward, frowning, his expression changing. There's resentment, anger in his eyes fixed on me. "I heard you talking to Padre Roque. I'm just trying to help—I don't want your dollars, señorita; those are not my ways." Quickly he turns to leave.

"Wait, please. Forgive me. I didn't mean—I was thinking about your time accompanying me."

"Time?" He laughs. "My time is worth nothing. Days are too long for an old man like me."

"Then you have time to come along with me?"

"Perhaps you should wait for your uncle."

"Don Teodoro Espinoza, Las Piedras," I repeat to myself. *"Gracias."* I extend my hand, which he takes after a moment. "Everyone knows Don Teodoro," he says. "He'll tell you all the good things you're anxious to hear about Don Francisco. You see, at the end, Don Teodoro was your grandfather's only friend."

"His only friend?" I murmur, noticing that for the first time, the man is smiling. I wonder why it's such a weird smile.

❦ 11 ❧

I cross the plaza toward the side where the taxis are parked in front of the hotel, the same three taxis I saw the day of my arrival. I approach a driver with a white moustache, who is wearing a Basque beret; he's reading the newspaper.

"*Buenos días,* I'd like to go to the house of Don Teodoro Espinoza. He lives—"

"I know where Don Teodoro lives, señorita."

"I'm going home first. It's too early to pay a visit. I just want to be sure you'll not be busy around ten?"

"I won't be busy, señorita. May I take you to your house? I can wait there." Folding the newspaper, he quickly gets out to open the door for me.

Like Tomás, the driver stops me from giving directions. He knows "where Don Pachito's house is."

At home, while having breakfast, I tell Josefa that I'd like to go to Grandfather's room once more before I return to Connecticut. "You know, to see everything again." Last night, when I tried to go up, the door to the stairs was locked.

"Of course, señorita. Doctor Victor instructed me to

keep the door locked. Just let me know whenever you wish to go up there."

Is it perhaps because of the valuable arms collection? I wonder as I go on buttering my *arepa* . . . or is it something else, some secret Uncle Victor wants to protect? I abstain from asking. Instead, I tell Josefa that I'm on my way to see a friend of Grandfather's.

She interrupts for an instant pouring coffee in my cup but doesn't ask me any questions.

After leaving the plaza, the taxi descends along a bright street of small, similar houses with windows shaped like pregnant women. At last I'm seeing a cobblestone street. A gentle breeze is blowing. I feel a sudden animation. It occurs to me that here the sound of the breeze carries words, like human whispers, as if San Javier is telling me the town's secrets.

"Good morning, Doña Lorenza," the driver calls. At the door of a house, an old silver-haired lady in a rocking chair is mending what look like a pair of men's pants. She's chatting with two women. One is at the window of the house next door; the other, across the street, holds a child in her arms. *"Buenos días, Alejandro,"* the three women answer in unison and burst out laughing. The driver also laughs. Farther along the street, a woman is nursing her baby on the steps of her house while a little boy watches raptly. A man comes up the street whistling, carrying a ladder on his shoulder. This shabby lane is not concerned with progress or change, I say to myself. This earthy street remains loyal to the old San Javier of my mother's descriptions.

"What's the name of this street?"

"El Callejón de las Sonrisas," the driver says.

"The Alley of the Smiles? Good name, I'm smiling." He turns toward me, and we both laugh.

As the car continues on its way down, the breeze turns into wind, blowing the papers scattered along the street. I can hear the river, a murmur at first that soon turns louder, thunderous. Ahead, in front of me, the meadow opens into an immense stage, showing solid brick and stone houses with white wooden fences separating the gardens, houses that seem to have grown there, like the trees and the grass, belonging to the landscape, like the river. They evoke tradition and dignity, bringing to my mind Tita, the woman I met at the Lozanos'. Farther in the background, amid the treetops, is a snow white spire of a chapel or a small church. Along the riverbank, wildflowers grow profusely, purple, pink, pale blues, and bright yellows alternating.

"What beautiful flowers," I comment.

The driver slows down, as if perhaps he's going to stop for me to get out and pick a few. Then he says, "Unfortunately, they cannot be picked."

"Prohibited?"

"No, no." He waves a hand. "Nothing is prohibited here. And these flowers by the river belong to everyone. It's just that no sooner do you pick them than they die. And what do you think of the butterflies, señorita? Can you see them? There, to your right."

I see a cloud of colors. I had noticed it, thinking they were flowers swaying with the wind. Now I see that they are butterflies of all colors and brilliance. They are not flying. Suspended in a circle, they undulate, courting the flowers. Wherever my eyes turn, I catch a glimpse of color and light.

Now on a level road, the car continues parallel to the river for a short while until it turns onto an unpaved road.

"Is that the place of Don Teodoro?" I ask, pointing at a red mansion.

"That's Las Piedras, señorita." The driver explains that the house behind, which is not visible, is a small replica of the big one. It was once the house of Don Teodoro's older son. "He was murdered years ago."

"Murdered! Why?"

He doesn't answer for a moment, then says, "An enemy of old Don Teodoro. One evening the killer was waiting in ambush for the old man, and the son came by, riding his father's horse. He shot the son, believing he was killing Don Teodoro. The killer gave himself up to the authorities but was freed. You see, his crime was one of honor."

"A crime of honor?"

"*Sí,* very common around here. Perhaps you haven't heard that this region, Santander, is known as the land of *hombres de honor.* Don Teodoro had violated one of this man's daughters . . . or the wife, I don't recall. There's no jail or punishment for crimes of honor."

Neither I nor the driver speak for a moment. I'm thinking of what Matesa told me: "Your grandfather composed songs about valiant men whose pride it was to defend the honor of their land and their women." Songs about crimes of honor? I can't help wondering.

"The other son, the younger one, lives in that house now. Don Torito," the driver is saying. " 'Little bull.' That's how everyone in San Javier calls him, Don Torito, because when he comes out of the cantina every evening, he's like a bull before the bullfight. You know, a bull before the fight is kept in total darkness. When the animal is let out for the exhibition, he's blinded by the light, stumbling into everything. That's Don Torito. There's a daughter, too, Señorita Alba. She takes care of the old man."

I'm recalling what Señor Lozano said about the father and daughter being despotic and unsociable: "They live like hermits and want to be left alone." Would I be received?

"Here we are," the driver announces.

"*Buenos días,*" the peon at the gate says, gesturing to us to drive in. He's throwing heavy sacks into a truck. My apprehension increases as the car advances along the gravel path leading to the house, which doesn't look all that impressive as we near it. One of the windows is broken, and the black paint on the door frame is peeling.

The driver gets out. He rings the bell and stands there, head bent, waiting. He keeps moving the fingers of his hand, as if he is about to play the piano. It's clear that he's also nervous. After a moment, a large, bony woman with a beaked nose half opens the door, looks at the driver, then at the car and frowns. A maid, I tell myself, but the driver bows, taking off his beret, calling, "*Buenos días,* Señorita Alba. I trust you're well."

The woman's face doesn't change as she mumbles something I cannot hear, keeping herself half hidden by the door.

"The señorita," he says in a loud voice, signaling the car, "is here to greet you and Don Teodoro. She arrived from the United States this week."

Arching her eyebrows, the woman smiles. It's not a friendly smile, rather a sneer. Anyone can read on her face the words she's not saying: Is that so? Well, we are not interested in visitors, no matter where they come from. "Who's there?" she asks finally.

As I see and hear everything from the car, my anxiety grows. Yet strangely, as I have done since I left home, I surprise myself by getting out of the car. I march toward the woman, saying, "My grandfather was Don Francisco Zamora. I've been told he was a good friend of your father, Don Teodoro."

Her eyes measure me from head to toe. "What's your name?" she asks at last. She hardly opens her mouth to address me. Perhaps speaking is an effort with which she doesn't want to bother.

"I'm Camila Draper."

The woman drops the hand that had been half closing the door, coming out at last. She begins pushing away the hairs from her forehead. Her angular face softens; her eyes acquire a shine; even the beaked nose becomes an asset to her countenance, which is gradually turning handsome. "You are not—My God, are you María Teresa's—Are you the daughter of my friend and the gringo? Draper, of course! That's the only foreign name I remember. Where is she? Come out of that car, María Teresa. Teasing me as usual, no?" Opening her arms in a welcoming gesture, Señorita Alba moves toward the car.

"No!" I grab her dress, detaining her. "My mother . . . she's dead." I cover my face quickly. The woman's transformation as she recognized me, her friend's daughter, brought Mama to life for an instant and an avalanche of tears I'm fighting to contain. "She died unexpectedly this past October," I add, wiping my eyes.

Señorita Alba stands there. Slowly, she draws a hand across her face.

The driver, now near the car, sniffles as if he's also weeping.

No one speaks for a moment. I have the feeling that the wind and the trees, the birds and the river, have joined us in momentary silence. Then I feel Señorita Alba's strong arms around me.

"Shall I wait, señorita, or—" the driver asks, turning the beret in his hands.

"Come back after lunch around . . . two?" Señorita Alba answers as she pushes me into the house. Turning toward the driver, she calls, "*Gracias* for bringing my friend's daughter."

❦12❦

We are both standing in the foyer. "I can see you are María Teresa's child. Yes, of course." She continues looking at me for a moment. "Your mother wrote to me often, at the beginning, you know, Camila. Didn't she mention me to you?" But she doesn't wait for my answer. "Then, perhaps María Teresa was resentful, and quite rightly. I never answered her letters. I'd hear from her once or twice a year. I even have a picture of you, Camila, when you were a baby. I don't know why I didn't answer. Perhaps envy kept me from writing, although María Teresa was careful telling me of her happiness, only small doses in each letter. And yet, in spite of not answering her letters, I've always kept in touch with María Teresa. On Sundays . . ." Her voice breaks for an instant. Speaking louder to control her emotion, she continues, "On Sundays after church, while I would go on my weekly horseback ride, I'd talk to María Teresa. I had nothing to tell her about my life, *nada*. I'd just go on mumbling reminiscences about the time when we were girls like you, and so close to each other." She sniffles with such force, she startles me. It's an angry sniffle, as if perhaps she's telling herself, Don't be a fool; don't cry now in front of her child.

She finally leads me along a hall with a wooden floor. The room to the left has the rug rolled against the wall. The house is sparsely furnished. It seems to contain only the essentials: chairs, tables, a grandfather clock. No adornments or vases with flowers can be seen anywhere, no pictures on the wall except a black and white portrait at the end of the hall of a homely gentleman, whose face is so devoid of life that the picture might have been taken when he was dead. The house reflects a total absence of vanity, like the clothes Señorita Alba is wearing—a waistless, blue-striped dress made of thick cotton, and on her feet, blue sneakers. She guides me in and out of rooms without saying which room is which while constantly talking. "This house was the hacienda. It had seemed then, when María Teresa and I were girls, so far from the town." She tells me also of the time when they kept a home in the plaza. "It was not lonely there, hearing the noises from the plaza, seeing from my window the Sunday Mass crowds, you know. Then Papa decided we should move. He couldn't remain there while San Javier was changing around him. He hates the changes."

We enter a small room with an orderly pile of newspapers on the floor. An older man sits in a chair close by. In his hands he has a large, postcard-size deck of cards, which he keeps shuffling with clumsy movements. I pause. A smile on my lips, I'm ready for the introductions, feeling both apprehensive and exhilarated to meet my grandfather's friend. Señorita Alba, however, pushes me gently to go on. The room is like a passage between the house and a hall that leads to the porch. The old man looks up at me, then grunts. His daughter makes a gesture with her hand, as if she were placating the family dog to stop it from barking at a stranger. I follow Señorita Alba into the wooden verandah, crowded with plants—a variety of ferns and other flora in pots on the floor, on iron stands, and hanging in baskets from the ceiling. A rocking chair and a straight-backed chair with a low table in between are the only furniture. On the table is a life-size white ceramic cat.

"Was that Don Teodoro?"

"That's him, yes. You'll meet him in a moment, after I talk to you," she says, plopping down in the rocking chair, showing me the chair opposite her. "How old are you, Camila? Let me guess—sixteen, seventeen?"

"Seventeen."

"Seventeen," she repeats softly. "I've spent most of my life fighting the memories of the time I was a young woman. And now, seeing you . . . everything comes back!" She throws up her head, laughing, perhaps at the irony of memories she evades that are now forcing themselves into her mind. I notice that she's missing one of her upper front teeth.

"I was young for a very short time, very short . . . Don't let me go on, Camila. Who wants to hear about the broken illusions of an old maid?"

"I want to hear. Please tell me, Señorita Alba."

She's silent, her large hands pushing away the strands of hair from her face. Then, one hand to her shoulder, she begins massaging it up and down. The bony shoulder seems to grow larger, misshapen, like the broken wing of a bird. That's what she looks like, I tell myself. Señorita Alba is like a huge bird, an ostrich. I can't take my eyes away, fascinated by the woman's ugliness and her beauty.

"Your mother was my best friend, why, my only friend, really. We were both very protected, attending only a few social events, although I can't compare our lives. Don Pachito was a good father, always considering the future of his children, sending them to the best schools, taking them abroad on vacations, all that. María Teresa and I were at that age, you know, when girls confide in their best friends. We swam in the river, we went horseback riding, we were always playing tricks on each other." She sighs. "Then one morning when she was to come and spend the day with me—that was at the time when our home was on the plaza—a maid arrived with a message. 'Niña María Teresa has left town.' Don Pachito had made arrangements to send her to boarding school in Bogotá, the maid explained. I cried as if I had lost my friend forever, and I had . . . María Teresa spent most of her teen years at the house of her aunt Doña Chinca, Don Pachito's sister, in Bucaramanga. But Mama kept consoling me, telling me that soon I would see María Teresa again. 'Any day, Alba, you'll see your friend.' All that happened before Doña Adelaida . . . Don Pachito didn't want either of the two children around."

My eyes are fixed on Señorita Alba, who keeps moving her lips but says nothing more. "You say, 'Before Doña Adelaida.' What happened with my grandmother?" I wait, but the answer doesn't come. "That Grandmother suffered from nervous breakdowns, that's all Mama told me about her mother."

"That's all? Maybe that was all María Teresa wanted to remember. I mean, your mother probably made herself believe all that talk about Doña Adelaida's nervous breakdowns." Señorita Alba shrugs her shoulders. "I got to know Doña Adelaida well when it was my turn to visit your grandparents. Sometimes I'd spend two or three days there in la Calle de los Naranjos. I liked to go when Don Pachito was away, attending a horse fair. Doña Adelaida liked me. She was outgoing and spontaneous, you know. Her manner somewhat inhibited the other women. She openly said she didn't like living in San Javier. Don Pachito would attend social events alone, but that story about your grandmother being *muy nerviosa* was an invention."

"What was wrong with her?"

"Doña Adelaida was a different model from that of San Javier's women. She had lived abroad for a while with her family . . . also in Bogotá. She felt out of place in this town. Then, after he prohibited—Mama used to say that it was an irony that of all people, the wife of Francisco Zamora would rebel—"

"You say 'after he prohibited'?"

"Doña Adelaida had a beautiful voice. When she came to San Javier as a bride, she sang at the picnics and at the club parties. That went on for a while. Then, unexpectedly, Don Francisco put an end to his wife's singing in public. He prohibited Doña Adelaida from singing."

"I don't understand. Why couldn't she—?"

"I'm sure it's difficult for you to understand, Camila. But you see, wives in those days were submissive; they were shadows of their husbands. Don Francisco did not want his wife to be different. Who knows, maybe he felt diminished as a man. She sang in church at the novenas and the evening benedictions, disobeying her husband. Mama told me that the church filled with people to hear her singing. The church was the only place Doña Adelaida visited."

" 'She sang and she prayed,' " I murmur to myself, repeating what Matesa had told me.

"I recall one occasion"—Señorita Alba makes a long pause—"your grandfather gave a traditional picnic every twentieth of July on Independence Day. Everyone traveled to his farm for the celebration. It was San Javier's social event of the year. An extravaganza that lasted three days, with dancing, horseback riding, the men hunting, all that. That year, after he prohibited her from singing, Doña Adelaida pretended to be sick. She left Don Francisco alone to be the host. That was a local scandal. More so because after that he stopped his tradition of the yearly picnic. People talked, the men mostly. It was as if Doña Adelaida's refusal to accompany and obey her husband was also an affront to them, the rest of the men of San Javier. If powerful Francisco Zamora could do nothing about his wife . . . you see? They were scared. There was a rumor that Doña Adelaida was a bad influence on the women of San Javier. At the end, Don Francisco's friends' wives also repudiated Doña Adelaida. Not my mother, I must say. She visited her clandestinely. We both liked Doña Adelaida. She was a loving mother, a pious woman. She was fun to be with. I recall those times at her house when Don Pachito was away, María Teresa and I laughing, Doña Adelaida, too, as we closed the windows so that the neighbors would not hear her singing and playing the piano. Doña Adelaida was different, but she was not crazy. She was not!"

We keep silent for a moment. "Mama lived with her mother; she must have known she was not having nervous breakdowns," I say softly, talking to myself. Then I burst out, "Why—why didn't my mother—"

"No more of this, Camila. I have so many questions to ask you and all I do is talk, talk . . . I haven't offered you anything. Ninfa!" she shouts, standing up abruptly, moving toward the door.

A wrinkled-faced woman with a slim, young figure and a red carnation in her hair comes in. She has a goiter the size of a tennis ball. "Today's juice is *chirimoya,*" she says, smiling broadly. In elaborate sentences, Ninfa describes how dull the orchard has been this year. Orange juice and papaya juice day after day. "This morning I said to myself 'Go find a *chirimoya* today.' So I walked through the brambles, their whips punishing me all along. See?" She lifts her long skirt to show her scratched old legs up to her thighs. "And there they were, hiding from me, or waiting for me, I should say." She bursts out laughing. The tale goes on and on. I gaze at Señorita Alba sideways, expecting her to interrupt, but she listens to every word, as if Ninfa is telling an absorbing story. It occurs to me that this inane conversation probably takes place between them every day, that Ninfa's long stories lighten up the two women's daily monotony. As Ninfa is finally ready to leave, Señorita Alba says, "We'll have the *chirimoya* juice with our lunch. Get busy, Ninfa. We have a guest." She points at me.

"I see, I see, and a very pretty guest," says Ninfa, swaying her slender body as she leaves the porch.

"What brought you to San Javier, *querida?*"

I explain about the commemorative pillar with Grandfather's name that will be placed in the plaza in his honor this weekend. "I received an invitation." I wonder if it's because Señorita Alba is unsociable, as Lozano said, that she doesn't bother to hide what so clearly shows on her face. She's smiling with the same cold mockery, the same irony she smiled with at the door when the driver was trying to impress her with news about a visitor from abroad.

"They're always finding some pretext for these celebrations," she says at last.

I feel unsettled by the tactless remark. "Are you telling me, Señorita Alba, that my grandfather doesn't—"

"What I think is not important, Camila."

"It's important to me!"

She smiles, her eyes looking at the distance, then says, "Someone used to say that to me once, long ago. 'Everything you say is important to me, Alba.' " She goes on nodding her head for a moment. "You see, from the beginning, since I was a child, I was taught that my opinions were for me to keep because I was a girl. The opinions that mattered in this family were my father's and my two brothers'. Then, when I was your age, at a picnic, I met a man, Roberto, who wanted to hear what I had to say and listened to me. Such was my astonishment that I lost my

97

head. I fell in love with him. He was an 'outsider.' That's how everyone in San Javier called Roberto. He was from the coast, a little town by the sea he often described to me. He was a soft-spoken man, a gentle person who did not carry a pistol and admitted to being afraid of them. Imagine! A man in San Javier admitting he's afraid."

"That doesn't answer my question about my grandfather not deserving—"

"It's all connected; let me finish." She moves both hands, asking me to wait. "For everyone in San Javier, this outsider was not a man; he was a coward. Roberto was even called a name I won't repeat. When he asked me to marry him, I spoke to my mother first. It took her many days and more prayers to find the courage to tell my father." She falls silent for a moment. "When she did, Papa talked to his best friend, your grandfather. Now you'll see why I'm telling you this long story. Don Francisco Zamora, with his influence, took my future into his hands. He immediately wrote a letter to the postmaster general, who had appointed Roberto as San Javier's supervisor of the mail and telegraph offices. In his letter Don Pachito said that Roberto Concha was persona non grata in San Javier, demanding his immediate removal from the job. So rapidly did your grandfather's influence work that Roberto and I were not even given the chance to say good-bye to each other."

I put a hand to my mouth. I am at last recalling Matesa telling me once about a dear friend whose life was manipulated by her own father, a close friend of Grandfather's, who forbade his daughter to marry the man she loved because he was not from San Javier. What my mother didn't tell me was the story of how Grandfather used his influence to have the man removed from San Javier. I burst out, "Just because he was not from this pueblo?"

"The true reason was that he was a soft-spoken, gentle man. Roberto did not conform to the standards of San Javier's *hombres*."

"But why—why?"

"Why what?" Señorita Alba touches my arm to calm me down. "Why didn't I rebel, why didn't I run away with him? I was seventeen, a girl educated with all honors in the school of submission. I know you can't understand it. I suppose I grieved too long for Roberto. Before I realized it, I was twenty-five. In those days, it meant I was an old maid. It also meant that my father and my two brothers could relax. They didn't have to be protectors of the girl of the family. That was always a nuisance that made men commiserate with one another." In a softer voice, as if speaking to herself, she says, "Maybe I shouldn't have said all this." She looks at me. "It's a long story, isn't it? But it answers your question, Camila. My sentiments for your grandfather, even now that he's dead, are not . . . It doesn't matter. My opinion doesn't matter, Camila. I'm sure María Teresa would have been pleased about this honor to her father. You should be too; that's what matters."

I am wordless. I try to imagine Alba's life in that big house alone. I myself am not a stranger to loneliness, without my mother, with my father always traveling, but my life is ahead, in another culture. I have a loving father. The comparison is absurd. Was Alba young only that year, when she was seventeen and felt loved by gentle Roberto? I look at Señorita Alba's mournful eyes, lost in that memory. I want to embrace her but feel shy. I put out my hand and squeeze Alba's hand. Didn't Grandfather know he was helping his friend to destroy his daughter's dreams, her life? Grandfather didn't know, he didn't know, I force myself to repeat.

"It's strange. One is able to get over the loss. What never goes away is the dream, the daily conjecture: How would my life have been if Roberto and I had married? How many children would we have had? Looking at you now, I think, would I have been the mother of a lovely daughter like Camila? The dream stays even at my age; it never goes away." She closes her eyes briefly, then laughs a forced laughter.

I will write letters to her every month, I promise myself, even if she doesn't answer me.

"I'm sorry; I have upset you, Camila. You may not believe me, but I am not a talker. Some days, you know, I don't open my mouth all day. But you must understand, seeing you, it's as if María Teresa is here with me and I am telling her . . . my dear friend." She gets up brusquely. "You want to talk to my father. Some days he's all right. Other times he's mumbling about the time when he was a healthy, strong man, and sometimes he makes no sense. You must forgive him if he's discourteous. This is his best hour. I'll give him a brandy; that usually tames him. Come."

13

"Papa, put away those cards. We have a visitor, the grand-daughter of your dear friend—"

"What friend?"

As Señorita Alba tries to take the cards away from his hands, they get into a struggle, he trying to hold on to them first, then amusing himself by letting the cards slide to the floor. I approach to help pick them up. "Behave now!" his daughter shouts. "We have a guest. This is—"

"I'm the granddaughter of your friend, Francisco Zamora." I extend my hand, which he shakes with surprising energy.

Señorita Alba leans over to the back of his chair. It's now, as I see her releasing the brake, pushing the chair out of the room, that I realize the old man is in a wheelchair. We all move to the large room with the rolled rug. "Camila is the daughter of María Teresa, who married the foreigner, an *outsider*," she adds, winking at me.

"Adelaida, Victor, María Teresa . . ." he says.

I smile, pleased at his recalling everyone's names.

"I'll bring you a cognac," Señorita Alba shouts, walking away. I sit on the straight chair near him. He looks at me steadily, my hair, my face, my blouse. It's a bold, intimidating look, improper for an old man. The tinkling of crystal comes from the next room.

"Here." Señorita Alba comes back with a small cognac glass filled to the top. "Careful." She lifts her arm as the old man's hand reaches up to grab it. "Don't spill it, for God's sake!" He drinks it all in one gulp.

"I want you to tell her about Don Pachito. She knows you were close friends and hopes you'll tell her something *nice,* a *pleasant* memory you have of him. She's *only* interested in hearing about your friendship with her grandfather."

I turn sharply, to catch the woman's glance, but see only her back as she's leaving. From the slow way she had spoken, emphasizing some words, it's only too obvious that Señorita Alba is instructing the old man not to say anything that might be upsetting. Not to mention Grandmother Adelaida? I wonder.

Don Teodoro grunts and goes on making a wordless noise, his eyes following his daughter.

She pauses by the door. "Not now. Behave and you'll get another brandy at lunch," she says with an air of satisfaction.

His fists closed, he shakes in his chair, grumbling, unaware of my being near him. After a moment, he says, "A disgrace to be old and invalid."

I don't know what to say, but I smile, half nodding, as if I am agreeing with him. "Were my grandfather and you the same age?"

"Damn no! Do I look that old?" He grunts, opening

and closing his fists. He's now also annoyed by my question. "Pacho wouldn't have tolerated that," he speaks at last, pointing toward the door where his daughter disappeared.

I want to prompt him to talk, but nothing comes to my mind. Although his shirt is clean, he has a dowdy appearance. I can perceive the odor of acrid sweat coming from him. His hair is yellowish white, messy, resembling clumps of overused cotton glued to the scalp, which would stand neither brush nor comb. He's strong for an invalid, like a mountain, but there's majesty, dignity in a mountain. He's more like a latent volcano.

"Pacho was older. He was the king and I was the page," he begins, chuckling. "That's the name people used for us, the king and the page. I didn't mind it."

Before I think of a comment, he says, "Pacho was the only man better than me in this pueblo. I learned with him. He was someone who inspired respect and fear." He pounds the arms of his chair with his fist to give emphasis to the last words, his small, watery eyes glaring at me intently.

I feel uncomfortable under his fixed gaze, yet I smile, encouraging him to go on telling me about "the king."

He shakes his head, saying nothing. I have the feeling that he's using all his energy to observe me.

"I hope you've received an invitation for this weekend, Don Teodoro," I break the silence. "Have you?"

"What?"

"You must speak louder, Camila." The unexpected voice of Señorita Alba comes from the next room. I had thought she was away in the kitchen. The clatter of silverware I'm hearing makes me realize that the next room is the dining room. Señorita Alba is probably setting the table for lunch. I wish I could be left alone with the old man. I begin repeating my sentence about the invitation.

"I heard you," he interrupts. "I don't hear the ugly old women living in this house, but your sweet voice I can hear." He gives a gurgle of laughter. "What's the invitation for?"

I explain about the weekend ceremony for my grandfather. "Señor Lozano sent the invitations."

"What does that salamander know about Pacho?" His lips continue moving, quivering, but no words are coming.

I have upset him again.

"I don't welcome invitations. That's the reason this house, which was the farmhouse, is now my permanent residence. The newcomers are building up the other side of town, destroying San Javier, that's what they're doing. I sold them my house on the plaza. They demolished it, replacing it with a monstrous edifice." He makes a long pause, balancing his body back and forth. "If Pacho were alive . . ."—he shakes his finger—"he would have thrown out that swarm of upstarts, the whole lot of them. Pacho always knew how to deal with outsiders and enemies."

"Did he have enemies?"

He winces, staring at me as if I have asked a stupid question.

"Have you ever known an *hombre* who has no enemies?"

"My father. He has no enemies. He doesn't agree with everyone, but he doesn't have enemies."

"He doesn't, eh? Bravo for the gringo." He claps, then laughs. His is a strange laughter. His eyebrows moving up and down, he's trying to convey something I don't understand but I sense is offensive.

Although I feel uncomfortable, I look at him intently. The sounds of steps and silverware in the next room have stopped.

"Was your wife a friend of my grandmother Adelaida?"

He takes a long time answering. His eyes turn smaller as he gazes into the distance. "That woman was a friend of no one," he says finally.

"Why was my grandmother a friend of no one?" I speak with urgency, afraid of hearing steps or seeing Señorita Alba back in the room.

"She was a stubborn mare. Not even Pacho was able to break her. She hated being here as if San Javier was hell. But Pacho—" He laughs. I have never heard a more disagreeable sound. It occurs to me that the old man has refined his laughter into a weapon. "Pacho was not a man to lose battles. I can still see him—Pacho that day, holding her arm, walking her, a bent, broken woman . . . the whole town watching."

My heart is jumping, wanting to get out. How is it possible, I reflect, that I want to hear and not to hear with the same intensity? Tell me, don't tell me, tell me! my heart screams. In too loud a voice, almost shouting, I say, "Tell me of a time when my grandfather was good and generous!"

"Generous? Don't you know? You understand what the word *benefactor* means? Pacho gave everything to San

Javier, the first hospital, the first school, a gymnasium when people didn't even know what it was for. Why, even the church bells. Before Pacho, when we were boys, the Mass and all church services were announced by beating a steel barrel, like the savages in the jungle. No one remembers that he made San Javier . . ." He mumbles a word I cannot hear. "At the end I alone was his friend. He died abandoned by the whole town—the ingrates. And you, his own daughter, you should know it."

"I'm his granddaughter," I whisper, as if I'm reminding myself. I wish I could get up and leave. How strange, I'm thinking; I came here to learn about my grandfather, and now I don't want to hear any more.

"How's your brother?"

"My uncle, he's coming on Saturday." I can hear the weariness in my voice.

"Your uncle, yes. What was his name?"

"Victor."

"Victor, yes. He was a disappointment to Pacho. Like his mother, Victor wanted nothing to do with San Javier. The boy was a weakling, nothing like his father. Why is he coming on Saturday?"

I don't bother explaining. "For the fiesta," I say.

"Fiesta?" he repeats, beginning to rub his hands.

The grandfather clock in the hall chimes twelve o'clock. Why is it taking so long for Señorita Alba to call for lunch?

Don Teodoro's small, gray eyes seem lost in some memory. "Pacho and I . . . Every Saturday we crossed the river in a canoe to the fiesta at La Casa de La Filomena to see the girls." He laughs his repulsive laugh.

The beats of my heart repeat, Don't tell me, don't tell me!

He's mumbling women's names, Josefina, Lola, Rosa, after each name another word. "Rosa, the frisky one."

It's clear that he's classifying the girls at La Casa de La Filomena for their physical attributes. Like horses, I tell myself. Although he's not looking at me, I see his hand moving toward me. Before I realize it, he lifts my skirt, his ugly hand creeping up to my thigh.

I jump to my feet, knocking down the chair, which makes a loud noise on the wooden floor. "Stop it. I don't want to hear what you and *he* did when you were young—"

"Young and old," says Señorita Alba, entering to find out about the noise.

I pick up the chair from the floor.

Bending her face near her father's, she says, "I knew you were eventually coming to that. Shame on you!" But she's rebuking him as if he were a child who did something naughty but harmless. "Who cares about two old men playing with the *muchachas* in the brothel."

"They prefer Pacho and me to the young men," he says, wrinkling his nose, making a funny face at his daughter.

I want to be alone; I need to collect myself. "May I use your bathroom?"

"Turn left; it's the little white door along the hall. Come back soon, Camila; the soup is on the table," she says, releasing the chair's brakes, rolling the old man to the dining room.

* * *

107

In the taxi, returning home, I make an effort to listen to the driver. Fortunately, he doesn't interrupt himself as he describes a coming parade. "The bishop from Bucaramanga, the school, the authorities." He enumerates the prominent locals who will attend the parade. At the end of each sentence, he looks at me through the rearview mirror.

I'm thinking of my visit to Don Teodoro's house, rebuking myself. I have committed an act of disloyalty toward my mother, Uncle Victor, my grandfather . . . everyone living and dead in Mama's family. Yet, was not this what I was looking for? That someone would tell me how great Grandfather was, as I heard it from Don Teodoro? To hear an anecdote that would bring him to life, as Señorita Alba did? At last I'm understanding the darkness, the gathering shadows I sensed behind Matesa's last stories about her father. Was Mama going to tell me the truth one day? Did she know the whole truth?

How uncomfortable I felt having lunch with Don Teodoro and his daughter. He calling her old woman, she denying him a second drink and a refill of his soup. As I witnessed the scene, it occurred to me that Señorita Alba, through her daily actions, takes revenge against her father for what he did to her life—with my grandfather's help.

"Will anyone from your American side of the family be here for the ceremony?" the driver asks me.

"My father will be here," I answer, realizing at that instant that the parade he has been describing will take place during the weekend celebration to honor my grandfather. I explain briefly that my father is on a business trip

108

in Brazil. "He was able to arrange his schedule and will be here on time." As I say it, I'm aware of my longing to see my dad. I'm recalling our discussion. He did not want me to travel alone, yet at the end he said what I wanted to hear him saying: "This is what Matesa wants. Make her proud of you in San Javier."

We have reached the plaza. "See, señorita?" The driver points at the center, where men are hammering and lifting planks. A small crowd, mostly boys, stands around watching. "That's the platform for the speakers."

"I see," I say, feigning animation.

"And the balloons and those rolls of colored paper are to decorate the trees around the plaza." The band, he tells me, will probably be rehearsing all day tomorrow, "and it will get us all in a fiesta mood." He turns to look at me, then begins boasting about San Javier's band. "It's the oldest band in all the region. It was formed years ago, at the time when your grandfather was a young man. The present director, Señor Ruffino, is an Italian, married to a Colombian. We're very proud of our band in San Javier."

"I see," I say. It seems to me that I have lived my life hearing about San Javier's wonders: the people, the climate, the landscape, "the valiant men defending the honor of their women and their land" . . . And as of Saturday, they'll have one more marvel to add to the list, the monument they were missing to honor their Illustrious Son.

I feel irritated by the driver, who keeps going around and around the plaza. He's pointing at the town hall, a white stone two-story house with a protruding, belly-shaped balcony. "The balcony," he says, "is associated with hypocrisy—the false promises of politicians who stand there, spitting lies. No prestige to that balcony." He laughs. "But the platform is different." He continues, "The First Authority orders the platform for ceremonies to honor *la patria.*"

At last, he turns toward the Calle de los Naranjos. As I'm getting out of the taxi, ready to pay his fee, he refuses to accept it. "It's my pleasure, señorita, serving Don Pachito's granddaughter today, my small contribution to this event that fills San Javier with pride." I insist, arguing about the time he has given me. I want to ask him if he has a wife, grandchildren to whom I can send something. Finally I say, "My mother often told me of the kindness of San Javier's people." Immediately I catch myself thinking, About this my mother told me the truth.

"We have a telephone at last!" Pepita rushes to meet me. "They installed it today." There have been several calls, Pepita continues, mostly for Josefa. "La Primera Autoridad, Señor Lozano, asking if everything is ready for Doctor Victor and his family."

"When will they be here, Pepita?"

"They'll be here tomorrow," Josefa calls from the dining room. She comes to the door, repeating, "Tomorrow."

"And one call for you also," Pepita says. "Señor Bernardo is picking you up at seven. He wanted to confirm it."

I had not thought about it all day, but I'm pleased at the prospect of seeing Bernardo. He's someone closer to my age. Mostly, he's someone who knows nothing about my family. He could not recall my grandfather's name when he introduced me to his friends.

I thank Pepita and walk to my room. This afternoon I avoid looking at the pictures around me. Today I don't feel welcomed by invisible presences. I shouldn't have gone to visit Don Teodoro and his daughter. Instead of coming to the land of my mother's family like a loving granddaughter, I'm behaving like an investigator, a condemning judge. It occurs to me that I am an intruder who has come to this pueblo, and into this house, to cast out the spirit of my grandfather. I pause near the bed for a moment, feeling remorseful. Then, as I'm about to lie down for a short nap, I turn to stand in front of the photograph where my grandmother is extending a protective hand toward the child with the butterfly bow, my mother. After what I heard from Señorita Alba, I know that the sadness coming from this picture was not in my imagination, that it is there, very real. "It's about my grandmother I want to hear," I murmur to myself. Yet I stopped Don Teodoro from telling me more about the "bent, broken woman." I was afraid. Now, in retrospect, I realize that it was not only fear. I didn't want that vulgar man to taint Grandmother Adelaida's memory. Uncle Victor, alone, will answer my questions—or will he? As I continue standing by the photos, I become aware that my eyes are avoiding the portrait. I cannot stand looking at the beautiful, lively young woman. I'm recalling Señorita Alba's words: "What never goes away is the dream." Did my grandmother also make daily conjectures about what her life would have been like had she not been in San Javier, married to a man who forbade her to sing? Was it Grandmother herself who spread the rumor about nervous breakdowns to keep away from San Javier's social life—or was it Grandfather who found it convenient to invent his wife's mental illness?

It's not difficult for me to accept that Matesa, as a child, believed everything she was told about her mother. Lying to children in order to preserve the prestige of the family name is part of this culture. But, as an adult, did Mama believe the lies about her mother? Was my mother going to tell me the truth one day? I ask myself.

❦14❧

Tonight I'm considering only my own pleasure and comfort as I get dressed. I am at last wearing jeans, a plaid shirt, and sandals. For the first time since I arrived, I'm dismissing the need to be "just right," as Mama would have been, for San Javier's approval.

In contrast, Bernardo is all dressed up in a suit, white shirt, and tie. His longish hair is held softly with an inconspicuous black ribbon at the back. I want to laugh as I see the surprise on his face, looking at me, reflecting my own surprise looking at him.

He rubs one of his temples. "We're going to the club, Camila. Maybe I didn't explain. You see, Thursday night is rather formal at the club. He turns his head toward the side of the living room, suggesting, I'm sure, that he can wait while I change.

"Couldn't we go somewhere else?" I suggest.

"Enrique made reservations for us." He looks down at himself. "And I—"

"Sit down; I'll be ready shortly."

Back in my room, I walk straight to the armoire. I pull out the hanger with the plastic protective bag, the ivory linen dress, to wear on Saturday, at Grandfather's ceremony. My father, who had never interfered with my clothes buying, contributed his opinion. I had packed the dress lovingly in layers of tissue paper.

"You'll be the beauty of the club tonight," Bernardo says as I come back.

I interrupt, saying that I'll be like Cinderella. "I should be home before midnight, Bernardo. Uncle Victor and his family are coming tomorrow, probably early."

He shakes his head, contradicting. "They'll be here tomorrow afternoon. Your uncle, your aunt, and one of the twins. The other can't make it. She's apparently—"

"She and Carlos, her husband, are expecting their first child," I explain. "How is it you know all this, Bernardo?"

"I try to learn about things I'm interested in. I asked Enrique. So you see, I can bring you back from the club late and you'll still have time to get ready for them. How about bringing you home at . . . dawn?" He bursts out laughing. "Don't make that panicked face. I'm just teasing."

He's attractive when he smiles. Like the first time I met him, I feel a certain magnetism coming from him.

The club is on the outskirts of San Javier. It's a moonlit night. I recall with a mixture of amusement and sadness how, listening to Mama's first stories about Grandfather galloping on his horse, in my child's imagination, every night in San Javier was a moonlit night. I have been throwing a veil of enchantment over everything since I arrived. I must stop seeing the world through Matesa's eyes. Tonight, in Bernardo's old, noisy car, I see the street and the houses as they are, San Javier as it is, a pueblo with no de-fined character. Bernardo is pointing at the golf course, which can be seen through the white picket fence, ex-plaining it's a nine-hole course and that the golfers in San Javier can be counted on one hand. "Years ago, Americans from an oil company in a nearby pueblo used to go to Bucaramanga to play golf."

I'm thinking about my father and mother. They had met at the country club in Bucaramanga while she was living with her Aunt Chinca. My mother often told me about that weekend. My father was a participant in a golf tournament at the country club. He was an engineer in the American Oil Company and lived in the camp on the Magdalena River in Barrancabermeja, the oil town in the state of Santander.

"Someone in San Javier decided to compete with Bucaramanga," Bernardo is saying. "So this golf course was built, and everyone had to pay for it."

As we approach the club, a sprawling country house sur-rounded by gardens, I can hear music.

"Are we meeting friends of yours?" I ask as Bernardo parks at the end of a long line of cars.

"Not for dinner. We'll see some friends later. By the way, Camila," he says, as he opens the car door for me, "you'll find the music tonight dull, easy to resist." He tells me that a group dedicated to preserving indigenous music will play. "You won't hear anything modern or exciting tonight."

"You mean *pasillos* and *bambucos?*" I ask, recalling Mama's favorites—soft, rather sentimental melodies played by guitars, mandolins, and violins. I don't tell him that modern, dancing tunes with drums and maracas are precisely what I don't want to hear this evening. Yet I'm not in the mood to listen to the *pasillos* and *bambucos* that Matesa played at home, which are connected to so many memories.

The waiter, following Bernardo's instructions, guides us to a romantic table in a corner, away from the musicians and dancing area. The tree outside, bending toward the window, is illuminated by the moon.

At a long table, not far from us, sits a family with several children and an old couple; both the silver-haired gentleman and the lady are wearing corsages with orchids.

Bernardo is different tonight from the inattentive person of the first night, asking me if I'm comfortable, ordering a glass of white wine for each of us. He begins a lengthy, uninteresting description of the club, the year it was founded, the reputation it has, "as one of the best social centers around." It's clear to me that the club is another source of pride for San Javier. I tell myself that perhaps the club is the reason for Bernardo's improved manners tonight.

"Enrique thought it would be a good idea to bring you here. Tonight is regional food night."

"How nice of him to think about me and of you to follow his suggestions."

Bernardo is silent while a smile spreads across his face. "You're often wrong, I've noticed. We had a date; did you forget? I asked Enrique for your phone number to confirm our engagement tonight. Both times I called, you were

116

out. Enrique told me you had gone to Don Teodoro's house, that you were very anxious to speak with him about your grandfather."

"How did he know I was there?"

"Everyone knows everything here. The plaza is the eyes and ears of San Javier's people. Awful." He rolls up his eyes.

"Were you born here, Bernardo?"

"No, but I grew up here. Now I'm anxious, ready to go away and see other places."

"Someone asked you the other night when were you leaving."

"I'm going to Spain, to the Universidad de Salamanca, to finish my studies there in architecture."

"I didn't know you were already a university student. I thought—"

"I should have finished my studies," he says softly. "I wasted time, traveling, playing music, drifting . . . a useless log in the river, as Papa said." He shakes his head. "You see, I was playing the flute in a local band, my head heavy with dreams. Well, I am twenty-eight. About time I—"

"Twenty-eight?" I understand now why Bernardo is different from the boys I have met. I feel a sudden inhibition, at the same time a new attraction toward Bernardo. He has become something forbidden, someone about whom I'll confide in my friends, not my father, of course. I won't tell Dad I had a date with a man of twenty-eight.

"Remember, Camila, what I said to you the night I met you, that I was speechless about your green-brown eyes and about something else that I would confess about later?"

"And that I hope you'll let me know tonight."

"That other thing was disappointment, not because you were not a blonde gringa, as you thought." He laughs. "But I was expecting someone older, closer to my age. And when I saw you, you looked lovely, of course, but so young, so innocent. I had a vision of a schoolgirl with pigtails."

"I'm sorry. That's why tonight I'm wearing my hair up so that you won't be ashamed of me."

"My disappointment turned into admiration." He looks at me intently while he nods. "I think that you, Camila, are one of the most mature girls I have known."

I feel myself glowing with pleasure.

The waiter brings the two glasses of wine, then places two menus on the table.

I take time reading the list of the *comida criolla*. For me the names of these regional dishes are words of a language I learned early, when I was a child. Every one evokes a memory, an image of our dining room in Connecticut: my father arriving from one of his trips, my mother waiting for him with one of the dishes he likes so much: *mute, arepa, guarrús, génovas*. These names even became popular with our neighbors and friends. Every year during Christmas, Matesa would give a luncheon for friends, consisting of typical Colombian dishes.

I'm suddenly aware that Bernardo and the waiter are expecting me to make a decision.

"Mute," I say, "with all the things that come with it."

Bernardo orders the same.

"I hope your visit to old Don Teodoro was . . . what you expected," he says, lifting his glass.

"It was a horror," I answer. He's looking at me, expecting to hear more. After a moment, I add, "I feel as if a roar of disapproval has been following me all day."

"Disapproval?"

"It sounds silly, but I'll take the risk of telling you—disapproval from my ancestors. And today, for the first time in my life, I was introduced to my grandmother, about whom I have heard so little. It's as if I were not supposed to love her."

"You sound resentful."

"I don't want to feel this way—nor do I want to bore you, Bernardo."

"Why are you so interested in hearing about your grandfather?"

"I'm not . . . anymore. I know *all* about my grandfather."

"Frankly, I find it tedious to hear family stories. I mean, whenever one of my aunts begins telling anecdotes about the past, I want to leave the room."

"I understand. I'm sure that if my mother were alive, I wouldn't have cared. I remember the times when I stopped her from telling me some story or memory from the past. But since I am here in San Javier, I feel . . ." I don't finish.

"You feel, go on."

"As if this yearning to learn about the past is the legacy my mother left to me. She was obsessed with her family, San Javier, her country. She passed her virus to me."

"What questions are you asking about your ancestors?"

We don't speak for a moment. Then I say, "If you were to discover something, Bernardo, let's say you find there's a mystery, some secret in your family that you unexpectedly have access to, would you want to know about it?"

He takes some time answering. "I *would* want to know, yes. Not so much because I'd be curious to find out, but because I'd think of my future regret. I mean, have you heard that of all remorses the worst one is not for the things you have done but for what you haven't done?"

"I haven't heard that," I say, without adding that I like it. "Your brother-in-law told me that there were many in this town who had forgotten Grandfather, even his name, while others remember him for 'the other thing'—those were his exact words."

"So?"

"I wanted to know what 'the other thing' was, the 'wrong thing' for which he's remembered. Now I—"

"Now you sound disappointed. Did you think your grandfather was perfect? Heroes and illustrious men with statues are not canonized. They're not like saints in the church, you know."

"Of course I know. But Mama made me think that her father was a great man. I believed her. She lied to me. Why?"

"Obviously, your mother loved him."

"Loved him so much that she never found feelings, I mean understanding, toward her own mother?" My quivering voice embarrasses me. Bernardo, looking at me, is trying to find something to say.

After a moment, he says, "Enrique is anxious to have everything go well this weekend. It's important for him. He's afraid there's not going to be a large crowd. He wishes he could do"—he interrupts himself to laugh—"what is done in small pueblos on election days—to fill envelopes with money and hand them out, instructing people whom to vote for, in this case bribing them to be at the plaza. What Enrique wants is to have a crowd of farmers and peasants from the countryside. He's afraid that only members of the social club and town hall employees will attend the celebration, that the whole event will turn into a social gathering rather than a patriotic commemoration." He pauses, still half laughing. "Am I saying the wrong thing, Camila?"

"Don't worry, I know the town is eager for an illustrious son." I laugh. Not recognizing my forced laughter, Bernardo joins me. "Pachito Zamora, I hate this Pachito name," I burst out. "Why not call him Francisco? That was his name. It seems odd to me that in this place, where men are superior beings, they chose this ridiculous diminutive of Don Pachito. Your brother-in-law," I begin, then stop. "I know that Don Pachito is an excuse; he's being used, isn't he?"

"I don't think so, but . . . who knows? Does that bother you?"

"What a question, Bernardo! Of course it bothers me. To have people giving speeches, praising this Don Pachito, who is remembered for 'that thing.' Did I come all the way from the United States to be part of a . . . a farce?"

"Camila." He grabs my hand, which I have been waving

while speaking, and brings it down to the table. "Dinner is here and I'd rather you tell me about yourself."

I'm glad to see our dinner: the plates with the aromatic *mute* soup, the small dishes with onions and garlic in tomato sauce, and the diced cheese, tripe, and crisp bacon to pour over the *mute.*

We concentrate on eating.

Couples are leaving their tables to dance. The musicians—two guitarists, a violinist, and a mandolin player—are performing a slow, melancholy piece. The dancers maintain the same walking step. They look as if they are strolling gracefully around the dance floor. Perhaps because the women are wearing mostly white dresses, and the men dark suits, I have the impression I'm seeing couples twirling in an old black and white movie.

"We'll dance later if you wish, Camila."

"I should be home early." I'm enjoying myself, yet I don't feel I am altogether here with Bernardo. I'm thinking of myself alone in my room, opening the leather box.

"Around midnight, this whole solemn atmosphere changes. The young people come in, bringing the right music. Then things liven up with the *invasión de los caníbales.* That's what we're called."

"The cannibals' invasion?" I laugh. "That's quite a name. Do you behave so savagely?"

"It's actually a fond name."

After dinner, we walk in the garden. The air is filled with the perfume of flowers and trees. Even the music from the loudspeakers has the right volume. Other couples are also strolling. A man and a woman standing on a miniature bridge are gazing intently into each other's eyes, aware only of themselves.

Bernardo and I glance at them quickly, then at each other. "Do you have someone special at home, Camila?"

"I have a friend I see often. We're not in love, but we enjoy each other's company and go to places together. He's working in Canada this summer. His mother is American, and his father is from the Philippines. We have things in common . . . mostly our insecurities."

"Insecurities?"

"We're both from two cultures, following two currents, keeping customs that often conflict and contradict one another, you know. At times it's like carrying a heavy load on each shoulder. That's how Marcos puts it."

"I'm sure here, in San Javier, you feel altogether an American, no?"

I nod, remembering something my mother often said: "When in Colombia, I feel I am an American. Then here, in the United States, I feel forever a foreigner."

"I hope you're staying long in San Javier, Camila."

"I'm leaving Sunday with my father. He'll be here tomorrow." I look at my wristwatch. It's almost ten. "What about you, Bernardo? You have someone, of course."

"Yes and no. I have had a rather long relationship, but you see, Maruja is just one year younger than me. She can't understand my turning into a university student and going away to Spain. She'd like us to get married, but I can't afford marrying now. So things are not going well between us."

We continue strolling for a while. Then he pauses near a

marble fountain with a Rubensesque cherub. Bernardo takes my face in both his hands as if he wants to examine it under the moonlight, turning it one way and the other, carefully, as if I were made of porcelain. Unexpectedly, he kisses my lips. It's a gentle kiss, brief yet intense. I long for his lips on my lips uninterruptedly, but just as his kiss took me by surprise, his hand on my arm now guides me to the parking lot.

We drive home in silence. All the way I wonder if he will kiss me again when we say good-night and if I should tell him that I have changed my mind and would like to be back at the club for "the cannibals' invasion."

"I hope everything will work out well between you and Maruja."

"Maruja is seeing someone else. I'm not included in her plans anymore." He drives in silence, seemingly absorbed in his thoughts.

San Javier's streets and houses are sharply delineated under the moonlight.

At the door of the house, he says, "Who knows what the future will bring"—he pauses—"for you and me."

"Friendship." I'm surprised to hear my quick answer. Why did I say this? I ask myself. He looks at me in silence. In his eyes I see the same concentration as when he told me that I am one of the most mature girls he has known. Is Bernardo's opinion of me what I want to preserve? I wonder.

"No me olvides, Camila."

"Nunca te olvidaré," I say sincerely. I've already framed Bernardo within my memories of San Javier.

He takes my hand and retains it for a moment, while his other hand presses the bell. Josefa opens the door immediately. Her expression turns disappointed as she sees us. Was she expecting someone else? I wonder. I thank Bernardo for the evening and walk in quickly.

I can't fall asleep. Uncle Victor and his family will be here tomorrow. Tonight is my last chance to see what is inside the leather box. Yet I don't want to think of myself opening the drawer of the sideboard, taking the key, and creeping into Grandfather's room in the darkness. While I'm having these thoughts, an inner voice admonishes, "Don't violate the past of your ancestors." I keep on turning in my bed. There's total silence in the house. From time to time, I hear the mournful hoot of an owl. Mama once told me about a local man whose pet was an owl, which he kept in a dark room. At night he would walk with the animal perched on his shoulder. The people of San Javier would run away, the women making the sign of the cross. "The man and the owl were considered messengers of Satan. Finally one night the man was thrown out of San Javier and his house was burned."

I'm now sitting on my bed, very aware of my decision. I will go upstairs. Once I get the box, I'll bring it back into this room, knowing that tomorrow, at my leisure, I'll look at its contents. I avoid turning on the lights while I tiptoe outside the room into the hall on my way to the dining room. I push the huge door softly. Thinking about the dark stairs, I hesitate for an instant. Then I turn on the lamp over the table. My eyes are fixed on the sideboard, yet I don't move to open the drawer. It's as if the key is the one thing that will identify me as a trespasser, an offender. I remain near the door for a moment, wondering if I shouldn't once and for all forget about this box, which might contain nothing that would concern me. Instead of moving toward the side table, I walk to the door that opens to the stairs. I turn the knob. To my surprise, the door is not locked. Josefa, dear Josefa, has left it open for me. Yet I am trembling. I notice that she has put a bulb in the small lamp on the wall at the foot of the stairs. I begin mounting. The hall with the hunting pictures is dark. I go on touching the wall until I find the switch. I hesitate at the door of the big room, avoiding turning on the ceiling lamp. Although Josefa is at the end of the house, she might see the light through the window facing the main patio. I move carefully, battling my fear, which grows with each step as I approach the closet. I'm perspiring cold sweat, and my own heavy breathing scares me, as if I'm being followed by someone. I move toward the side where the little bathroom is, grateful that I had left the door ajar. I turn on the light. The blanket-wrapped package with the mandolin and the toys are just as I left them on the floor of the closet. Quickly I search for the box at the back. Gripping my treasure, I leave the room, switching off lights, leaving only the bulb on the stairs.

I am at the bottom of the stairs, closing the door that separates the stairs from the dining room, when I hear the sound of a car and voices coming from the front of the house. Bernardo? I wonder. Is he returning to ask me to join him and his friends at the club for "the cannibals' invasion"? The doorbell is ringing. What a nuisance! Josefa will come in an instant to open the door. I stand there paralyzed. I hear soft steps in the entrance hall. And then I understand. Who else would have a key to the house but Uncle Victor? It's clear that he opened the door and rang the bell simultaneously to let Josefa know that they have arrived. Oh, God, please help me, help me, I pray. I can't decide between running up the stairs to hide inside the closet or crawling under the dining room table. I decide to sneak upstairs. As I open the door and grab the bell attached to the back to stop it from ringing, the leather box falls, spilling its contents on the dining room floor. Steps and whispering voices are already in the main patio. Dear God, help me, I pray again. Although Josefa, as well as Aunt Natalia and Uncle Victor, are all greeting one another in whispers, their voices resound like thunder in my ears, intensifying my terror. "Shall I awaken Señorita Camila?" Josefa asks. There's a brief silence while I wait breathless.

"Let her sleep. We'll see her tomorrow," Aunt Natalia answers.

"And you, Josefa, go back to bed," Uncle Victor adds.

Josefa tells them she has made hot chocolate and fresh *pan de yuca,* which she baked that afternoon as soon as she learned they were coming tonight. "You must be hungry," she insists. My uncle and Aunt Natalia go on deliberating in whispers. I know that in an instant Josefa will stride across the patio to open the dining room door and turn on the light. I am on the floor, half of me under the table. I understand now why people can die of terror.

"I love your yucca bread, Josefa. Let's have some,"

Monika says in a loud voice while everyone hushes her to keep quiet.

"You're going to wake up Camila," Aunt Natalia says. "It's past midnight, Josefa. We should all rest now for what's coming." I hear their soft giggles. I'm recalling Josefa's disappointed face when she opened the door to Bernardo and me, thinking it was Uncle Victor and his family. She knew, of course, that they were coming tonight. Everyone is tiptoeing away from the main patio. I remain immobile, my body twisted on the floor. In the darkness, to which my eyes have become accustomed, I can see envelopes and shiny squares that, I guess, are photographs. I wait for a long while until silence returns. Then I get to my feet, turn on the pale bulb on the stairs, and pick up the envelopes and the photographs, pushing them back into the leather box.

In my room, I finally begin to examine what was inside the box. The large envelope is addressed to my grandfather. I look at the photos first. I instantly recognize Grandmother Adelaida. In one of the pictures she's very young, perhaps fourteen. With her hair falling over her shoulders, she's wearing a white dress and is pulling a curtain that opens to a balcony. Half biting her lips, she has the expression of a girl caught in mischief. All the photos are of Grandmother Adelaida with an older girl. One shows the two seated at a table, leafing through what appears to be a photograph album; in another, Adelaida's head is resting on the older girl's shoulder. They are both wearing wide skirts and lacy blouses. I realize now that the other girl is my grandmother's older sister. Matesa often mentioned her aunt Nelly. She's tiny and pretty in an old-fashioned way, with delicate features. Her face resembles that of an angel in a holy picture. She doesn't evoke the liveliness of my grandmother. I put the photos on my night table, then take the thick envelope. I slide out what appears to be a letter of several pages. I hesitate. Finally, as I unfold the pages, I see a covering letter:

Francisco: I'm enclosing two letters concerning my sister Adelaida that I preserved all these years. If you take the trouble to read them, you'll understand your crime. Your sister-in-law, Nelly.

I drop the letter on my lap. The word *crime,* written in larger letters, jumps at me from the paper. My eyes are glued to the word. It can't be true. "Grandfather did not commit a crime," I hear my own whisper, while the bed makes a noise trembling under me. I don't believe Nelly's accusation, yet I cannot push away my dark thoughts, my suppositions . . .

I'm holding the two attached letters. Fear overcomes me. I don't dare to read Grandmother's letters, yet I look at them at random:

. . . I understood at last why Francisco would not speak to me . . .

My eyes jump ahead and I read:

You see, Nelly, everything I do is wrong. I talk and laugh, I read and cry. Worst of all, I play the piano and sing.

Perhaps because of the late hour and my scare a few moments ago, I feel incapable of going on reading tonight. I wish I had never come to San Javier. I don't want to be a part of this coming homage to Francisco Zamora, my grandfather, whose name alone now causes me terror.

I begin folding the pages, inserting them back into the envelope with the photos. I have an odd feeling that someone else is taking the box from my hands and placing it softly on the night table. "Mama," I murmur, "did you know about these letters? Were you going to tell me . . . one day?" Finally I turn off the lamp. I'll read Grandmother's letters tomorrow in daylight. For a while I go on listening to the silence of the house and the pounding of my heart.

15

The tender tree stands alone, unprotected in the midst of a prairie under a gray sky, which threatens a storm. The wind will strip the tree of its leaves and branches, leaving it exposed—a solitary, bent, graceless pole.

I still have the drawings of the tree from a project in grammar school depicting the four seasons. My artwork had won a prize. Sister Rita had seen in my tree a symbol of a youngster confronting life alone. My picture and the other winning pictures were exhibited in the halls of the school for a month. After Mass, my parents and I would walk the school hall, admiring the paintings. Then Papa would take us for Sunday brunch to an old colonial country house overlooking Silver Mine River.

The day is bright. The sky over the patio, where I am now standing, is so radiant it lightens my heart, softening my memory of last night. This morning, while I heard Josefa and Pepita moving about, knocking on my door, Josefa calling me *La Bella Durmiente*—Sleeping Beauty—I rushed to hide the leather box inside the armoire. As I wait for Uncle Victor, Aunt Natalia, and Monika to come out of their rooms, I tell myself that what I have been feeling toward them is mostly anxiety about their reaction upon seeing me for the first time since my mother's death.

Now, feeling their arms around me, I am relieved by their silence, yet somehow, I'm hearing their words—the words I want to hear: "You have us, we love you," making me feel I am an important member of their family. Arms around one another, we walk toward the dining room. I feel strengthened in their presence. The tree, I'm thinking, is not a solitary winter tree but a blooming spring tree.

The table is filled with all of "El Doctor's favorites," Josefa says. It's a brunch, since everyone got up late, skipping breakfast. In unison Uncle Victor, Aunt Natalia, and Monika compliment Josefa, who, standing by the door, shakes her head, waving a hand at them. "Nothing worked the way I wanted," she says again and again, looking apologetically at Uncle Victor.

"This is what you always say, Josefa, after you create your wonders," Uncle Victor replies.

"Where are you going, looking so pretty, Pepita?" Monika asks.

Pepita has a white dress and a large pink bow on her ponytail.

"To the plaza. The band is rehearsing again today." She smiles, lifting a hand to her mouth.

"All these celebrations for Don Pachito are affecting her brains," Josefa says, pushing Pepita softly. The two leave, closing the door behind them.

Aunt Natalia tells me about their clandestine arrival last night, eluding Señor Lozano, then bursts out laughing. "We told him we'll be here sometime in the late afternoon." They all laugh, their faces mischievous as children's. "We told Josefa not to tell anyone. We wanted to spend the day with you alone, Camila."

Uncle Victor explains that it was impossible for him to leave his patients until yesterday. "I was at the hospital until the last minute."

"Monika and I would have come to join you, Camila, but I didn't want to leave Lalita—I have a feeling that our first grandchild will be arriving just when we are here."

"You have been saying that over and over, Mama, since we left Bogotá," Monika says. She has a new hairstyle, a poodle cut, which accentuates her high cheekbones and pouty mouth. She and her twin sister, Lalita, whose name is a shortened form of Adelaida, are a contrast in character. Monika has always been the controversial one. "She reads too much; she'll never find a husband." I recall my parents laughing as they read Aunt Natalia's repeated sentence in her letters. Monika is too outspoken, in the family's opinion, her remarks forever fluctuating between compassion and cruelty. Lalita is a docile girl, a constant talker, never saying anything to be remembered. The twins are twenty-three.

It's difficult to speak as we go on passing dishes to one another, filling our plates.

"You disappointed us, Camila." Uncle Victor makes a long pause as he observes his wife filling his plate with an herb omelet, rice, meat patties, and ham. He continues, "We were all expecting you'd be with us these past days, before this thing tomorrow."

"I'm sorry, Uncle."

For a moment the only sounds are made by the plates and silverware and Monika, who exclaims how good everything looks and smells.

After wine is poured, Uncle Victor lifts his glass. "First, to María Teresa, whose absence is . . ." As he looks at the empty place by his right side, his lips continue to move but say nothing. Slowly, the glasses are lowered, then he lifts his glass again, keeping it up in the air for an instant. We all drink, our thoughts together on Matesa.

I imagine my mother here with us, near Uncle Victor. I can see her, with a happy expression on her face, wrinkling her nose slightly and encouraging me to smile. I look at my uncle, sure that he's going to make a second toast, perhaps mentioning tomorrow's ceremony.

Lifting his glass, he says, "For having Camila with us today."

"Thank you, *Tío.*" Unintentionally, my eyes dart to the portrait. "What do you think of this picture, Uncle?"

"I think it's very good—Lozano is trying his best."

Monika says, "To my grandfather, the Ambassador."

"The Ambassador?" I ask, thinking, Something else I never heard, perhaps something I stopped Mama from telling me. I say, "To my grandfather, the . . ." I'm appalled by the thoughts coming into my head. My grandfather the criminal, as his sister-in-law called him? My grandfather the manipulator who destroyed Señorita Alba's life? I'm at last aware that they're all looking at me, waiting. "To my grandfather, the farmer," I say quickly.

Aunt Natalia puts a hand across her mouth. She's laughing. "Isn't that typical, Victor? The Ambassador . . . the farmer."

"He was not an ambassador in the proper meaning of the word, Camila," my uncle explains. "Once, long ago, he was a member of a committee of horsemen traveling to Mendoza, Argentina, representing Colombia. The press called him and the ones going with him ambassadors, and for a while everyone in this town referred to him as the Ambassador."

"I'm disappointed," Monika says, turning to her mother. "I've always referred to my grandfather as the Ambassador. That's what you told me, Mama."

"That's why I couldn't help laughing, the contrast between María Teresa and me. You see, we made our choice. It's like the comparison you, Victor, and I often make with these earthenware jugs." She points to the center of the table, at the jug holding the wine. "They change their color to the color of what you pour into them. If it's milk, for instance, they turn white, and now, look at the jug with the red wine. See what I mean, Camila? It's red."

"So you poured plain water in your jug, Mama, making me believe that it was wine," Monika says.

"And I should add something else, Camila. Your grandfather was not a farmer either," Uncle Victor says.

"He wasn't?"

"He came from a family of farmers, grew up on a farm, but he really was never one himself. After his parents died, he sold the farm, invested in horses, and began his own horse business."

"Are you mentioning something about this in your speech tomorrow, Victor?"

"It's not a speech, Natalia, I told you," he says, a hint of impatience in his tone. "I'm just going to say *gracias,* that's all."

Both his wife and Monika tease him about his speech. Is he going to wave his arms like a politician? Will he have a mike? They go on asking questions, making fun of him affectionately.

I look at him. I recall that the first time I met my uncle, I was apprehensive of him. Although he was very affectionate to me, he seemed too retiring for a Latino. Then when he came to visit us in Connecticut the last time, I was older, more mature in my opinions. I saw that he was reserved, preferring to give attention rather than to attract it, as Mama had often described him. He was easily moved. I recalled that when saying good-bye to Matesa, he did not hide his teary eyes. He's a small man, in comparison with his wife, Aunt Natalia, a husky, handsome woman, always erupting with laughter, "calling things by their name," as Matesa described her, fondly referring to her sister-in-law as *La Amazona.*

"Seriously, Victor, you must include some lively little story in your words tomorrow, an anecdote."

"Anecdote? Better to leave anecdotes out. Some men's lives revolve around one single anecdote."

"What anecdote revolves around Grandfather, Uncle?" I ask, my heart accelerating.

He doesn't answer while we're all looking at him. Finally,

he says, "Perhaps you don't know the words of Ecclesiastes, Camila?

*There's a time for everything, a time to speak
and a time to be silent."*

"These days here in San Javier have been very . . ." I want to say "painful." Instead, I say, "Very confusing for me, Uncle Victor."

"I didn't think much of your coming here by yourself, Camila. What exactly was your point? This is a small town filled with rumors, a place like all pueblos, where gossip flourishes."

"I shouldn't have come by myself. But you see, Uncle, I wanted to be in San Javier, to feel closer to Mama and—" Grandfather, I finish my sentence mentally. I would not tell my uncle about my visit to Don Teodoro: *"A time to be silent."* I apply the quotation to suit my convenience. "I'm afraid I've grown up believing in fairy tales."

Aunt Natalia and Monika smile. Uncle Victor is looking at me with his usual thoughtful expression.

"There's nothing wrong, Uncle, in wanting to know the truth, is there?"

"The truth," he repeats. "Nothing is more relative than the truth, Camila. We, each one of us, build our own illusions as well as our truths."

"I'm like my father. For me truth is fact, reality, a thing as it is. That's what I want."

"Like a good American girl," Aunt Natalia says.

"I agree with you, Camila," Monika remarks. "I also get

impatient with this constant juggling of lies and truths in our country."

Juggling, I repeat to myself. I'm recalling the dream about my grandfather. I've never forgotten it: The ugly little man onstage, his hands moving up and down, tossing things in the air, retrieving them again. A juggler of lies and truths, of virtues and vices . . . A juggler of human fates? The last thoughts come unexpectedly, as if they have been lurking within me, waiting in ambush all these years.

They are talking now about my father, "El Gringo," as they call him affectionately.

"I didn't want William to be uncomfortable in this house," Uncle Victor says. "I made reservations for him at the Hotel El Regazo. It's a place with a good reputation. Of course, William will have his meals here; he'll be with us all the time. I wouldn't be surprised if we see him any moment." He looks at his watch.

"I'm sorry that Dad will not be staying here. I like this house, my room!"

Uncle Victor and his wife exchange glances, clearly disagreeing with me.

"This is an old, uncomfortable house, Camila, a house"—he puts out his hand to tell his wife he doesn't want any more on his plate—"a thoughtless house, built for the convenience of one person." His eyes dart to the portrait. "Bedrooms without closets, no playroom, not even a porch where you can relax or read the paper or have a conversation—only that small, dark living room. It's a house with a bathroom that requires an exploration trip." His voice has taken on an angry tone. Aunt Natalia pats his hand.

"Surely you must have a few pleasant memories from the time you were a young boy."

"I was a young boy when I was sent away. First, with the Christian Brothers to Zapatoca, then to Bogotá, finally to Europe. *He* was uneasy with us, with me mostly. You see, I never believed, not even then, in his argument about the need to keep this house shrouded in solitude and silence." His hands are resting on the table, while he looks down at his half-empty plate. There's a slight tremor on his face. He seems to be making efforts to control himself.

"Camila, you must think your uncle is an ogre. This is the way San Javier affects him. He'll get over it, won't you, dear?" She touches his arm.

"Señor Lozano said that you want to sell this house."

"I'm not sure, Camila. Your mother wanted this to be a place of reunion for our two families." He pauses for a moment. In a louder voice he adds, "Some renovations should be done to it. It's your house also, Camila. After Aunt Chinca died, the house passed to María Teresa and me. Your father and I have exchanged a couple of letters on this matter. I intend to ask William for suggestions. We should begin with the maids' quarters. Those rooms are an embarrassment."

"I know. I've been there. If, as you say, Uncle, this house is also my house, nothing would make me happier than to see Josefa's and her mother's and Pepita's rooms improved. Can we do something?"

Uncle Victor assents, smiling. "We'll certainly do something, Camila! They deserve to have their own apartment."

"I also saw Josefa's mother. I know this isn't done here—"

"Josefa told me last night that you had been there," Uncle Victor interrupts. "Her mother was our maid for all her life, really. There are no people like her anymore, Doña Josefina. She was so devoted. She loved my mother and served our family with loyalty. Josefa is just as good. She comes every month and spends a week or so cleaning, washing the linens, gardening. She told me it is like a vacation for them to be here." He shakes his head. "She brings her mother and daughter with her."

"I didn't know Josefa had a daughter."

"Shhh." The three hush me to lower my voice.

"Pepita—can't you see the resemblance?" Monika asks.

"This was *another* tragedy for the old woman, Doña Josefina. Her only daughter, Josefa, having a fatherless child," Uncle Victor says softly.

"Everything in this place is so melodramatic, really!" says Monika. "All right, the woman had a child and now what? Is Pepita to be an orphan, a 'niece,' with an invented story about her origin, always 'the niece,' and nothing more? Come on."

"No need to get so upset, Monika," Uncle Victor rebukes.

"I agree with Monika. Does Pepita know? Or will she one day be told who she is?" I look at my uncle first, then at Aunt Natalia.

"You two don't understand," Aunt Natalia explains.

140

"Your world is different, but this is the way it was before your time."

"Humble, decent people like Josefa and her mother had only one treasure in their lives, their honor," Uncle Victor adds, with finality.

Monika shrugs her shoulders as she takes an olive.

I meet my uncle's eyes, fixed on me. "Don't feel confused. Camila, don't try to go to the bottom of things. Life is not something like the stones and the trees by the road. There are enigmas we never understand. We'll talk, Camila; if not now, some other time."

"I want to hear *now* that I'm here, Uncle. I have questions—"

"Surely María Teresa told you about our confusion while growing up and how Papa kept us moving from place to place like gypsies. She was close to Papa."

"But you see, I must tell you . . . After all, you're my family." My voice breaks. I clear my throat to keep my voice from failing. "In the two years before she died, I didn't want to hear any more about her past, you know, my grandfather and San Javier. It's awful, I know, to have refused to listen to my mother's stories."

"It's not awful at all. It happens to everyone, Camila," Monika murmurs.

"Matesa had plenty of time to tell me whatever truths she had to say about Grandfather, but she didn't. She preferred to tell me about this utopia of San Javier—fantasies. I always knew that one day in the future, I was going to ask her to tell me more. It's like—like someone who leaves a play after the first act, thinking she'll come back again to

141

see the end. What a stupid comparison." I feign laughter. "And then you know Mama died suddenly—and all my questions . . ." I finally allow my voice to break. Quickly I put the napkin to my face.

Everyone dashes to my side. Solicitous, they surround me, Monika putting her arm around my shoulders, Aunt Natalia pressing my hand.

"I'll tell you everything you want to know, Camila, I promise," Uncle Victor says, kissing the top of my head. He walks quickly out of the room.

Shortly after lunch, the house begins filling with people. First, Lozano walks in with two men who call Uncle Victor's name and greet him as an old friend.

A moment later, Yolanda Lozano and her friend Alicia, both bringing flower bouquets, are in the living room, waiting for Aunt Natalia, who rushes out of her room to welcome them.

The furtive travelers arriving at midnight have been discovered.

"Camila! Monika!" Uncle Victor calls.

Everyone except Monika is now outside in the patio.

To my surprise, Uncle Victor as well as Aunt Natalia seem delighted with the visitors. Both are smiling, nodding at the suggestions: The men will be going to the town hall to discuss final details for tomorrow's function, the women on a shopping excursion to San Javier's outskirts, to a small market called El Kiosko, where Aunt Natalia wants to buy a few typical objects of the region. Of course, she has the *botijas* and *alpargatas*—the earthenware jugs and hemp sandals—she says, but would like to get a few more. She apologizes for Monika not being there. "Monika probably has her nose inside a book."

"A book?"

In a low, dramatic tone, as if making a shameful confession, Aunt Natalia says that "the girl is really addicted to reading."

"Reading?"

But Monika, who has heard all about the shopping excursion, is wearing a white cloth hat and has changed into a blue skirt and white blouse. "You're also coming, aren't you, Camila?" Monika asks.

I have been standing near one of the fern pots, waiting for the right moment to disappear into my room. I'm eager to be alone. I'm also thinking about my father. "Dad may call at any moment, and I want to be here," I explain.

"You'll be bored by yourself, Camilita," Yolanda says. "Enrique can arrange for someone to meet Mr. Draper."

Everyone is speaking at the same time, voices growing louder, competing with the band, which is rehearsing "The Blue Danube." The instruments sound so loud that I wonder if perhaps Señor Lozano has given orders for the musicians to move the rehearsal from the plaza to our street.

"We'll be back shortly, Camila," Aunt Natalia says, kissing my cheek. "Please listen for the phone. I have the feeling that our grandchild will be arriving just when we're here," she tells Yolanda and her friend.

I am relieved to see everyone leaving. I rush to my bedroom.

"See what Pepita did, señorita?" Josefa says, delaying

me at the door. "She couldn't wait to run to the plaza. Then, a moment later she's back crying, telling me she doesn't know how it happened, but she told everyone that Doctor Victor and his family had arrived last night. You just saw what happened—everyone coming to visit and interrupt—"

"Don't worry, Josefa; they are all happy."

"Last night, Doctor Victor and I had a talk. He told me we can stay here for as long as we want." She moves closer. I can see that Josefa is in a mood for conversation. "He'll do nothing about the house until he talks to you and your father. What a relief. You see, señorita, our rooms here are not much. Doctor Victor calls them holes, but in comparison with our place, this is a palace. That's why I have my mother here, where we have water and all the services."

I can hardly contain myself from telling Josefa what Uncle Victor said at brunch about improving their quarters. I want to reassure her that my father and I will approve enthusiastically Uncle Victor's idea that they deserve to have their own apartment. I feel, however, it's my uncle who should give her the good news. I turn to go into my room.

"I'm excited today, señorita. Aren't you? We are all proud of these celebrations for Don Francisco."

I'm impatient with Josefa's ceaseless chatting and with the band, which has changed from "The Blue Danube" and is now playing a dance number, the music so loud it shakes the house. Yet in the background I can hear a soft, steady lamentation.

Josefa moves away from the door. "Can you hear, señorita? She senses everything that has to do with this house, this event tomorrow. The continuous sound of the band yesterday and today is upsetting her. She has been telling me she'll comb my hair . . ." Josefa smiles, closing her eyes briefly. She lowers her voice. "She tells me that the señor ordered her to leave my long hair loose," she concludes.

"The señor? She means Grandfather, doesn't she? Your mother is remembering an event with the two of them, my grandparents?"

Josefa nods.

I have the feeling that perhaps today Josefa would answer my questions. But I don't insist. I want to go inside the room and read Grandmother's letters. I put my hands on my forehead. "I'm going to take a rest," I say.

I wonder why Josefa is looking at me and smiling. Then as she moves away, I hear the front doorbell ringing. I rush ahead to open the door.

My father is standing there. "I'm so glad to see you, Dad, so glad. You're here at last." We embrace, remaining together for a moment. "Uncle Victor and everyone are out," I tell him, holding his arm, walking him into the house.

"I know. I saw Victor briefly. He stopped by the hotel to check just when I was at the desk getting my room key. They're waiting for me, for some kind of rehearsal for tomorrow."

"You—rehearsing?"

Papa is silent, looking around him for a moment.

Is he thinking about Mama, I wonder, imagining her here, the three of us together?

After a moment, his face again animated, he says, "Actually, I'm supposed to take your place at the rehearsal, then I'll explain to you what you have to do tomorrow at the ceremony."

"Come on, you're teasing me, Dad."

"No, no, seriously. They also want me to perform my famous—you know." He opens his arms and lifts a leg, twisting his head to one side, imitating a ballet dancer. It's something that has always made me laugh.

"You're a great clown, Dad," I say, realizing that for the first time since Mama's passing, he's performing one of his pantomimes.

❦16❧

I walk into my room, closing the door, locking it from inside, then to the armoire to get the leather box.

Dearest Nelly:
   Francisco is away, attending a fair, and María Teresa and Victor are sleeping.
   I remember how you always understood my silences, Nelly. You complain that in my letters I say nothing about myself and Francisco, or this house and my life in San Javier. Do I still sing at parties and picnics? Have I forgotten, you also asked me, that you were my confidante, my older sister to whom I rushed every time I had something good or bad to tell? How can I forget it, Nelly dearest?
   Remember how for a while I went on writing you that I sensed that something in myself, my ways, did not please Francisco, that I prayed every day that he would let me know what I was doing wrong? What I didn't tell you was that I understood at last why Francisco would not speak to me about what displeased him. You see, Nelly, everything I do is wrong. I talk and laugh, I read and cry. Worst of all, I play the piano and sing.
   Francisco finally spoke. He prohibited me from singing. "You must stop embarrassing me in public, Adelaida." He mentioned the wives of his friends, "quiet,

147

pious women." Why couldn't I be like these model
wives of San Javier? "I didn't marry an entertainer,"
he told me.

Now I sing only in church, at the daily Mass. To avoid
awakening Francisco at the early hour of Mass, I sleep in
my own room, close to the children's. Often, if it
doesn't interrupt my time with Victor and María
Teresa, I escape to church in the early evenings,
accompanied by my dear maid Josefina, to sing at the
rosary hour. So you see, Nelly? Now I am neither
the wife Francisco wants me to be, nor am I the
Adelaida you remember.

I often think of the day I met Francisco. We were
celebrating Papa's birthday, his last birthday . . .
remember? We were all gathered with friends and
relatives on the lawn of our house. I can still see the tables
set under the oak and tamarind trees; the musicians
playing in a corner; the maids, in their white
uniforms, rushing about with trays. You were already
engaged to Luís. Your hand lay on his arm as he guided
you around. I remember thinking that you two didn't look
like mortals, that you were different from everyone
else. To me, you and Luís were like angels floating
on the lawn among the trees. That Sunday was the first
time Francisco had come to our house. Felipe, or was it
Juan?—one of our brothers had invited him. Why
was I so instantly captivated by this short man with
a black moustache that, like a curtain, concealed his lips
and half of his teeth when he smiled, this little man, who
looked older than all the other handsome men
seeking my company? As usual, that afternoon I was
asked to sing. Someone handed me my guitar. Francisco
disappeared for a moment. I don't think anyone noticed
his absence, except me. He returned, carrying a
mandolin. He took a chair in his other hand and
placed himself by my side. When he began playing,

148

accompanying my singing, he seemed to me the most irresistible man in the world. As I went on with my guitar and my song, I was dreaming about the two of us together, he playing his mandolin, I singing. Life seemed to me so easy and beautiful, so moldable to my desires.

I have not told you this before, but here in San Javier I often surprised myself with feelings of resentment toward Mama and Papa. They made us believe that the world was our stage, a place where we were to be made happy and celebrated, a garden where we were the most delicate and beautiful flowers. I know, dear sister, I shouldn't reproach them. They were right about you, Nelly. I know how happy you and Luís are, how you enjoy living abroad, enlarging your knowledge of people from a different culture. My life in San Javier is a contrast. Some days I feel this house is my cell. And, should I tell you? I entertain myself imagining ways of escaping with my two children. Where? What an absurdity! Who would open a door to me, a deceiving wife, *una mujer mala,* as some people in this town refer to me? But enough about this. Why go on about things that have no solution? I did write a long letter to our brother Juan describing to him my life with Francisco. After weeks he sent a note, rebuking me, reminding me of my wifely duties, exhorting me to follow your example. "Like Nelly," he wrote, "you also must honor our name."

I don't want you to think of me as a sad, miserable woman, Nelly. I have moments of intense happiness. Just looking at Victor and María Teresa, hearing their voices, spending time with my two children, compensates me with a happiness I didn't know could exist. Francisco is often away selling and buying horses, attending fairs. On these occasions I play the piano and sing, while the maids run to close the windows

149

that open on the street, becoming accomplices to my sin, *este horrible pecado de cantar.* Without saying a word, we all laugh and dash about, excited by our clandestine misdeed. Perhaps you were right when you teased me, saying I was forever going to be a fluttering, singing bird. That's how I want you to think of me, Nelly.

Almost every weekend Francisco joins his friends, the husbands of these "quiet, pious women, the model wives of San Javier" he wants me to emulate. They go across the river to La Casa de La Filomena. On Sundays he sleeps all morning. This gives me the opportunity to go to early Mass with my children and the maids.

Now I must finish this long letter. I've told you everything that can be said through a letter, my dearest sister. How I miss you!

The last sentence of the letter is half erased, as if a drop of water or a tear had fallen on the ink, leaving only: *". . . my two children, the reason for my living."*

It seems to me that my heart is beating as noisily as the drums of the band outside, while I sit on the bed, holding Grandmother Adelaida's letter. I try to imagine her life in this house, feeling as if I have been in this room at that time with her, as if a fragment of me, her granddaughter, was witness to her loneliness and despair.

I now hear the voices of my father and Uncle Victor coming into the house. "I'll tell you everything you want to know, Camila," my uncle promised. Is he going to tell me his own fabricated truths? I wonder. I know I will not go back to Connecticut without confessing to him that I took this leather box and read the letters. That will put an end to his version.

As I begin to unfold the second letter, I see immediately that the handwriting is not my grandmother's. Quickly I turn the pages to find out the signature: José Roque Serrano, pastor of San Javier Parish.

Estimada Doña Nelly:
 Forgive my delay in answering your letter. You've endowed me with a responsibility that involves some risk. One might say that Don Francisco, your brother-in-law, is the owner of this town. My duty, however, is to God and the truth. I waited for a propitious occasion to visit your sister, which I did this past Tuesday, a day Don Francisco was away from San Javier.
 Doña Adelaida was not surprised to see me, believing I was there to ask why she had stopped singing at Mass. Like many in this town, I knew that Doña Adelaida's daily participation at Mass and evening rosary was not entirely an act of piety but mostly an act of rebellion against her husband. Don Francisco, learning, no doubt, that the church pews filled with people coming to hear his wife, decided to deprive even our Lord of Doña Adelaida's beautiful singing.
 You must not worry about the mental health of your sister, Señora Nelly. Her mind is sharp and clear, in spite of all the rumors around San Javier. She seems, however, very distressed. Doña Adelaida suspects that Don Francisco intends to send the children away before they finish grammar school, the girl to a convent, the boy to a school in Zapatoca. Separating her from her children, Doña Adelaida confided to me, is the best way of turning a lie into truth, for she feels she'll go *loca* without her children. It's a well-known fact in San Javier that Don Francisco refers to his wife as a mentally sick woman, incapable of taking care of his children. I tried to provide her consolation, asking her to

151

have faith in our Lord. While I spoke, she shook her head, dismissing my words. As her pastor, I also worry about her soul. As of late Don Francisco attends Sunday Mass with María Teresa. His friends, seeing him every Sunday entering the church, holding the hand of his small daughter, comment, "*Pobrecito* Francisco has to take care of his children because his wife, Doña Adelaida, is *loca*." No one really believes it. No one, however, dares to commiserate with your sister, to say, "*Pobrecita* Doña Adelaida."

I conveyed to her how worried you are, hearing nothing from your dear sister in so long a time. I also told Doña Adelaida how you dream to make that distant voyage from Paraguay with your husband and your girls. Hearing this, she said something I must quote to you: "I hope Nelly and her family will be able to come before my husband decides my fate, as he decides that of his sick horses." Had Doña Adelaida said this before, when she was the lively, humorous señora who sang and played the guitar and piano at all social gatherings, I would have given no seriousness to her words. Unfortunately, Doña Adelaida is now a silent, melancholy person. Before leaving, I made her promise that she would write to you.

Answering your letter, *estimada* Doña Nelly, I feel I have done what is my duty, as a pastor and a friend of Doña Adelaida.

> Yours in Christ,
> José Roque Serrano,
> Pastor of San Javier Parish

17

It's a bright day with the usual blue sky and gentle breeze of San Javier. From my room, I can feel the activity in the house, although there are no discernible sounds. It occurs to me that what I'm hearing is my own tension, like a roar in my ears. I have been up since dawn, washing my hair, drying it, taking out my dress from the layers of tissue paper in which I wrapped it again after wearing it to the club with Bernardo. I'm anxious for the ceremony to be over soon. I have the feeling that today I'll be on a stage to play a part with other, far more experienced actors. I'm not sure how well I'll perform my role as Francisco Zamora's granddaughter. Never before, not even after Mama's death, have I felt as lonely as I feel now. What distresses me more is the absence of my mother within me this morning. I've always sensed Matesa, as if in some corner of my soul Mama had remained alive, a force, a companion forever present by my side. Today I feel empty. I want to call her, as I did when I was a small girl, coming back from school, entering the house, "Where are you, Mama?"

Josefa is now announcing that there's juice and coffee.

153

Her voice has a crystalline quality. She's excited about the news Uncle Victor gave her last night concerning the apartment that will be built for her, her mother, and Pepita.

"Camila," Monika calls from outside my door. "How about some *curuba* juice or coffee?"

"I'd love some juice, Monika."

A moment later, Monika is in the room with a glass of *curuba* juice for me. She's all dressed up, ready for the day, in a glowing white suit that accentuates her dark beauty. "You look lovely," we say to each other in unison, then laugh together at our simultaneous compliment.

Monika looks around her. "So this is the famous room you like so much."

"Don't tell me you haven't seen it before!"

Monika says she has seen it, of course, but doesn't recall anything special. Maybe because she always rushed in and out. Her parents always made it their bedroom. She's looking at the furniture, the armoire, even up at the ceiling.

I point to the pictures on the wall, but Monika has moved to the table to take the hat Papa suggested I should bring for Grandfather's function. She tries it on, rushing to look at herself in the dressing table mirror.

"It looks great on you and goes with your suit, Monika. Wear it. I feel better without a hat."

"Are you sure?"

We both go on touching the hat. I pull it down on Monika's head, as the saleswoman did when I tried it on. Monika pushes it to the back of her head, finally taking it off. "You know, Camila, this is going to be a long, tedious thing. Maybe we can sneak out after the main event happens."

"I'd gladly do it, Monika, but I'm here representing Mama. I should be there throughout the whole ceremony."

"I know," Monika says, putting on the hat again, turning her head from side to side in front of the mirror. "Are you sure—you think I should wear it?"

How is it possible, I wonder, that Monika has no curiosity about the pictures on the wall? But wouldn't I be the same, had Mama been alive now? I know that I would have been rather indifferent, and perhaps I would have laughed at the picnic groups; the women smiling coyly at the photographer; the men's contrived postures, a hand in their pocket or holding a cigarette. I now notice Monika's eyes on Grandmother Adelaida's portrait.

"Papa thinks that you look like her, Camila—your eyes, your hair. He says that something in your expression is like Grandmother's."

"Really? I'm flattered. I think she was beautiful. Look at the other picture, Monika. The one where she's with a little girl, my mother."

Monika follows my finger and moves to look at it more closely. After a moment, gazing again at the portrait, she says, "This is yours, you know?"

"The portrait?"

"Papa ordered a copy for you and Aunt María Tere—I mean for you and Uncle Bill."

"I love it; I'll put it in my room. I've felt very close to her these past days," I say, thinking about her letter and how each word is engraved in my soul.

Monika moves back to look once more at the small picture of her grandmother. "Poor thing. She had a beautiful voice. Aunt María Teresa told you, didn't she? Grandmother Adelaida studied voice at the Conservatorio Nacional in Bogotá, where only the best voices were trained by experts brought from Europe. You can feel that something is wrong with her in this picture."

For a moment I'm tempted to show Monika the letters. Then I realize that this morning, just before the ceremony, is not the time to do so. "I *know* that Grandmother wasn't crazy, if that's what you mean, Monika. She was different, but she wasn't crazy, she was not!"

"I know she wasn't," Monika says, a sad expression on her face.

"Mama always told me about Grandfather: *He* did this, *he* said that. She always had something to say about Grandfather, hardly anything about Grandmother."

"But she couldn't, Camila. Aunt María Teresa and Papa were separated from their mother when they were in grammar school. Even when they were smaller, Grandfather was always taking the two of them on trips, leaving his wife at home. Then, when Papa and your mother were very young, he sent Papa abroad and Aunt María Teresa to his aunt Chinca's house in Bucaramanga. Papa said they really lived with their mother for a little while. When they came for short visits, Grandfather was always with them. The last time Papa saw his mother, before going to Europe, it was very sad. Grandmother Adelaida tiptoed into his room, the night before he left, to wake him up at midnight. She asked him to get up and dress quickly, that she was going to wake up María Teresa also, for the three of them were running away. Papa said that, for the first time, he believed that perhaps it was true that his mother was crazy."

I wait for Monika to say more. After a moment, I ask, "What else did Uncle Victor tell you, Monika?"

"Papa told us everything when he found the portrait, at the time of Aunt Chinca's death. I suppose it brought memories back to him, you know. The portrait was at the bottom of a trunk, with old shoes and rags, things to throw away. Can you imagine? Aunt Chinca apparently was convinced that Grandmother was *una mujer mala,* a cruel wife who had made her brother the unhappy, lonely man he was at the end. My mother knows the whole story, of course. Well, I'm sure you do know that Grandfather never forgave Grandmother for snubbing his beloved town, which was her way of ignoring him, *el gran hombre* of San Javier." Monika makes a long pause, as if she's not going to say any more.

"Go on, Monika."

"She never accompanied him to any of the social functions, not even to Sunday Mass. She was a good mother but . . . she made herself inaccessible to her husband, you know. He couldn't take it at the end. Papa said it was a matter of honor for his father to not tolerate that behavior from a woman, his own wife. He was being accused of losing control. Finally Grandfather called her two brothers. Her parents were dead. Well, Grandfather called the brothers and asked them to wait for him at the plaza after twelve o'clock Mass. That he had serious business to resolve with them. It was Easter Sunday. He wanted to be sure that everyone in San Javier who counted would be there, watching. And that Sunday he returned Grandmother Adelaida to her brothers."

"Returned?"

"His purpose, Papa said, was to save his dignity, his manhood, all that stupidity. The reason he gave to the brothers was that Grandmother Adelaida could be neither a wife to him nor a mother to his children. That she was"—Monika puts her index finger on her temple and twists it—"that she was *loca*. And there, in front of everybody, after Mass, he walked her by the arm down the church steps to the four-horse carriage where her brothers were waiting."

"I know, I know." I cover my eyes.

"I thought you said you didn't know."

"I know," I go on repeating softly. I'm seeing the bent, broken woman and the man, my grandfather, the Illustrious Son of San Javier to whom the town is paying homage today. Have I not seen it over and over, I ask myself, since the moment Don Teodoro said it? No other image has ever been so vivid, so piercing, than the image of my broken, humiliated grandmother being repudiated by "Pacho, who was not a man to lose battles," in the words of his friend Don Teodoro. "What happened to our grandmother after that? Did she ever see her children again?"

"Don't let this spoil your day, Camila. You must under-

158

stand this is the way things were then in this pueblo. They still are, I suspect, although Papa says it's changed now. You can understand why Papa detests coming here."

"What happened to her, Monika?"

"To return a wife to her family, Papa explained to us, was only done when the woman had committed adultery. So the brothers pretended to believe the story that she was crazy. After all, that did not soil their name and honor. They made it as public as possible that Grandmother was a virtuous woman, only the poor thing was *loca*." Monika closes her eyes for an instant. "That's the story of our grandmother, Camila." She puts an arm on my shoulder.

I take a step backward, as if my cousin's touch would keep me from finding out the rest. "Did they keep her in their house? What did they—"

"That's what Grandfather thought. Papa always says that he was sure the brothers would take her home. You're too upset, Camila. If I had known . . . Really, why are we talking about this? Today of all days." Monika moves away to get a Kleenex for me.

"Tell me, Monika," I insist. "You're my cousin and my friend; tell me. I need to know." I put my hands on Monika's shoulders to prevent her from moving farther away.

"She was kept in a locked room at the back of the family's house for several years. Then the brothers probably got tired of their responsibility. Grandmother Adelaida was committed to an insane asylum. She died there."

✂18✂

I'm standing between my father and my uncle. Aunt
Natalia is to the right of her husband, and Monika is next
to Papa.

Photographers from the local newspaper and a newspaper from the state's capital insist that the Zamora family
remain in their places for the photos, which will be taken
throughout the function. A young woman photographer
keeps stepping on her long skirt as she moves about, clicking her camera unobtrusively. My father and Uncle Victor
glance at each other. I can detect both impatience and
amusement on their faces.

Finally, the photographers are asked to finish and leave
the platform. The ceremony is about to start. It's at that
moment that I see Padre Roque. Close to him is the
young, handsome bishop, who advances to the front of
the platform. Putting out his hand, he motions for silence.
Then, extending both arms over the plaza, he invites everyone to join him in praying the Our Father. After a brief
speech in which "Illustrious Son" and "gratitude" are
clearly enunciated, the bishop descends from the platform, followed by an altar boy, who is carrying a silver

bowl with holy water. The bishop blesses and sprinkles the pillar, which is shrouded in green burlap. The band is playing the national anthem.

I look at Padre Roque out of the corner of my eyes. Head bent, eyes lowered, the old priest seems totally devoid of human curiosity. "I still hear her songs while I say Mass . . ." I recall his words and his courageous letter to Grandmother's sister: "My duty is to God and the truth." I stir with sympathy for the priest.

To our right, Señor Lozano, his wife, and other couples congregate. Everyone is dressed up, looking like guests at an elegant wedding, the women wearing straw hats with bands of silk flowers, Aunt Natalia with a pale gray fedora. I seem to be the only one not wearing a hat. There are no chairs for anyone.

The band is now playing a recognizable march, Sousa's "El Capitán." The conductor, a short, stout man, bounces. So vigorous are his exertions that his small feet occasionally lift off the little wooden dais where he stands. One hand conducts with the baton; the other hand opens and closes, as if simultaneously grabbing and tossing the quick, energetic notes of the march. The church bells and firecrackers have become a nonstop noise, with the accompaniment of barking dogs.

But all this uproar does not hide the fact that, apart from the musicians in their vivid blue uniforms and red kepis and the orderly double rows of the children from the public school, all dressed in white, few stand in the plaza. It is a small crowd.

There was another day when the plaza was filled with

161

spectators, I am thinking, one Easter Sunday long ago. Were the balconies of the houses around the plaza filled with women and children watching the event that, like today's, was also motivated by Francisco Zamora? "No one in San Javier has forgotten Doña Adelaida, no one!" Again I recall Padre Roque's words.

I can feel my jumping heart. It's a palpitation that alarms me, as if I were the carrier of an explosive weapon. I'm divided into two people: One is my mother rejoicing for the ceremony taking place; the other is me, rebelling.

The band, the church bells, the firecrackers, and the barking dogs stop. Señor Lozano murmurs something to his wife, then proceeds to leave the platform. With slow, solemn steps, he moves along the path leading to a small but higher platform, installed for the speakers. It's profusely decorated with tiny national flags and yellow, blue, and red ribbons hanging from the branches of the oak tree. He takes a paper from his pocket. Clearing his throat, he begins: "Your Excellency"; he bows in the direction of the bishop, then hesitates, perhaps considering if he should also address Padre Roque, who remains in the same frozen position. "Ladies and gentlemen," Señor Lozano shouts. One by one he mentions Victor Zamora, Aunt Natalia, Monika, me. "María Teresa, his late daughter, whose presence we all miss today, and Meester Draper, her widower, who interrupted his busy schedule to join us for this important celebration." Extending a hand toward the pillar, he pauses. Contrary to what I had imagined, the pillar is not a slender, tall column but small and squat. It occurs to me that, with the folds of the burlap cover, the pillar has the appearance of a very small man, a dwarf hiding inside.

"This is an historical occasion to commemorate and honor Don Francisco Zamora, affectionately called by his friends Pachito. Today I'd like to reverse the metaphor. Instead of saying that the great man we honor today is the Illustrious Son of our town, I'd like to say that Francisco Zamora was a loving, devoted father to San Javier, bringing his town step by step to the proud, modern position it occupies today—" Enthusiastic applause interrupts his words. One by one, Lozano enumerates "Don Pachito's donations and accomplishments." This time I'm listening to contributions I had not heard of before, such as "the building of our church." The morning I went to Mass to speak to Padre Roque, I read a metal plate attached to the main entrance: "This church was built in the year of our Lord 1742." After each donation on the list, Lozano is interrupted with applause. Slowly it becomes clear that Lozano is taking advantage of this endless list to launch into another litany: his own accomplishments as mayor of San Javier. He goes on with a description of his projects in progress, which takes considerable time. "To turn San Javier into the dream of Francisco Zamora." The long speech ends at last with "My efforts of these past years in my position have been inspired by the man we honor today, Don Pachito." After the applause, Lozano returns to the guest platform, close to his wife, while everyone shakes his hand, congratulating him for his speech.

The band begins anew, and with it, the firecrackers, the church bells, and the barking dogs.

163

My father puts his arm on my shoulder and presses me lightly toward him. I tense. I want to say, "Please, Dad, don't make me aware of what's going on. Pretend I am not here." I wish I could fall into unconsciousness like Padre Roque. But I put my arm around his waist, the way my mother used to do. Images of my parents flash through my mind: taking a stroll after dinner . . . Sunday afternoon excursions around the countryside . . . standing at the back driveway, waiting for the limousine to take him to the office or the airport—the tall, thin man, the petite woman, their arms around each other. I look up at my father, whose face is turned toward me, and we both smile.

A schoolgirl with long black hair now advances toward the speakers' podium, accompanied by a lady, perhaps one of the teachers. She's eleven or twelve. At the top of her head a white ribbon holds a crown of short ringlets resembling a bunch of black grapes. In a loud, high-pitched voice, the girl begins reciting a poem—or is it a prayer? I wonder, as I hear repeatedly, "Señor, oh, señor. You, the greatest man." Then as she screams "Illustrious Son," I realize that she's reciting a poem eulogizing Grandfather. The girl goes on for some minutes mouthing adjectives, all rhyming with *ilustrísimo*. At last she bows and comes down.

Long applause accompanies the girl until she finds her place in the line with the other students.

Not everyone here is playing a role, I think. The girl who just left the podium and the rest of the schoolchildren believe in this homage. Perhaps my father, too, the innocent

American. Is he also believing this comedy? I have the feeling that in spite of all the affection that Uncle Victor and the family profess for my father, he has been excluded from this occasion, left out, like the privet hedge outside the gate encircling Francisco Zamora's house. They probably would like him to believe that his father-in-law was indeed an extraordinary man.

I can feel my uncle's restlessness. In his hand he has a folded page with the words he'll say. Lozano, turning to him, calls softly, "It's your turn," gesturing for Uncle Victor to begin moving toward the speakers' platform.

Aunt Natalia's eyes follow her husband. Her face reflects concern. Eyebrows lifted, lips tight, her expression is one of apprehension, as if her husband is about to embark on a dangerous mission—a jump on a motorcycle, some risky stunt that might send him to the hospital.

Could it be, I reflect, that Uncle Victor is going to say that he, as well as his family, feel uncomfortable with today's celebration? Will he say, "Don't make my family and me instruments of your political game. Go find yourselves another Illustrious Son." I'm breathing hard, exhilarated at the prospect of my uncle's coming words, his courage. Mama often said that he was known for being outspoken. What is my uncle thinking as he advances, all eyes on him? Is he thinking about his mother that Sunday, long ago?

I close my eyes for a moment. I'm seeing my grandmother dressed in white, her long hair loose, more in character for the "insane" woman whose fate had been decided by her husband, "as that of his sick horses." Why am I seeing Grandmother so clearly? How do I know? It's as if San Javier, in the sound of its breeze, has been whispering to me the events of that Easter Sunday. Was Padre Roque amidst the multitude in that day's spectacle? Did he say, "Doña Adelaida's mind is sharp and clear"? Or was his "duty to God and the truth" only words to write in a letter? "There are remorses clinging to the soul like bloodsuckers—remorses one carries to the tomb." I give a start as I recall his words, understanding at last that Padre Roque was referring to himself, his own cowardice and repentance. What was my grandmother, "a bent, broken woman," thinking as she advanced to the center of the plaza with her husband gripping her arm while "the whole town was watching"? Was she thinking, Will I see my children again? Was she pronouncing their names? Involuntarily I whimper.

My father puts an arm around my shoulder, pressing me against him. "It's all right, all right," he whispers, thinking I'm crying for Mama's absence.

I clear my throat.

As soon as Uncle Victor reaches his place on the podium, the band stops playing, but the church bells continue. All heads look up at the bell tower. Don Cristóbal, the sacristan, probably feels this is his turn, his one chance for a solo performance. The tolling heightens with paranoiac furor. Lozano's eyes are fixed on the bell tower first, then on the bishop, who seems enchanted by the concert, a benevolent smile on his face. Padre Roque, by his side, has shrunken to the size of the pillar. Lozano wrings his hands. Finally, rushing down the platform, gesticulating, Lozano approaches one of the musicians, who runs across the plaza to accomplish his mission.

On the podium, Uncle Victor opens and folds his paper. Strangely, the incident with the bells seems to have relaxed him. He smiles as he waits.

People are shaking their heads; many are finding it difficult to control their laughter. In contrast, Lozano's face and the faces near him have become more solemn. I turn toward Monika, who is biting her lips, hat pulled back. Perhaps to avoid looking at others, she's gazing up at the sky.

At last, the bells cease. Silence falls over the plaza. Uncle Victor addresses the bishop, then says the traditional *"Damas y caballeros,"* and begins: "Perhaps the bells should have gone on as a background to my words." He's interrupted by laughter in response to his joke.

"Francisco Zamora's devotion to this town," he continues, "was the stream that nurtured his life. That's what we are celebrating today. This plaza has been the stage to numerous religious as well as patriotic and political acts, which are a component of San Javier's tradition, its history." He pauses. In a louder voice, he says, "Often in the history of pueblos, as well as in that of families, there are undesirable . . . shameful events. This plaza of San Javier has also been witness to injustice and human frailty, to cowardly acts that have tainted our local history, leaving indelible scars." He pauses. It occurs to me that for the first time the participants are truly silent and attentive. I sense a change around me, as if daylight had ceased, darkening the whole plaza. There's also agitation, like a turbulence rippling on the side of Señor Lozano's group.

"It has often been said," Uncle Victor proceeds, "that in our country statues to heroes burst forth like bushes along the countryside. San Javier, nevertheless, needed a monument, some tangible symbol to pay tribute to one of its sons. I am pleased that my father is providing this last service to his town." He slips the piece of paper he has been holding into his pocket.

Is that all he's going to say? I wonder, hearing the long pause. My inner scream demands that my uncle defend his mother, tell everyone the truth about his father.

"My family and I are grateful to Enrique Lozano and his assistants for their time and generosity in the preparation of this homage," my uncle ends, bowing and turning to walk down the ramp. His hair flutters in the breeze, giving him a momentary boyish look.

I'm disappointed, angry about my uncle's insipid speech. Is the male population of San Javier composed of weaklings like my uncle and Padre Roque and machos like my grandfather and Don Teodoro?

Señor Lozano is now near Uncle Victor, instructing him to remain near the pillar. Then Señor Lozano returns to the platform, where Monika and I are waiting. Placing himself between us, he takes our arms to escort us toward Uncle Victor for the unveiling of the pillar.

Drums alone now play a brisk staccato that makes me think of circus drums when a perilous jump is about to be executed.

Two men strip the burlap cover from the white marble pillar and its stone base.

The name Francisco Zamora and the dates of his birth and death are engraved at the top. Below, in large incised letters, it reads: IN MEMORY OF FRANCISCO ZAMORA, ILLUSTRIOUS SON OF SAN JAVIER.

❦19❦

Tonight, we are all reunited around the dining room table having coffee and *pan de yuca,* yucca bread. We're tired, silent.

After early Mass tomorrow, Papa and I will drive to Bucaramanga to catch the plane to the coast, and from there the flight back home.

My father gets up, excusing himself.

"I'll walk to the hotel," he says, patting my uncle back into his chair. "Stay where you are, Victor. I'm looking forward to taking this walk by myself." I go with him to the door.

"You must feel proud, Camila," he says. He has been saying the sentence all day long. Each time I have managed not to reply. It's clear that he expects me to acknowledge his words at last.

"I don't know if I should feel—I never knew my grandfather."

He frowns and looks at me for a moment. Then, throwing his head backward, as he does when he's displeased, he says, "So? Perhaps in your judgment, today's ceremony in his honor should not have taken place?"

170

"Oh, Dad, please. You don't know many things."

"I know *everything*, Camila. There were no secrets between your mother and me. I also know that Matesa found forgiveness in her heart for her father."

"I see," I mumble, thinking, Everyone knows—the secrets were only for me. "I can't believe I had to come all the way to San Javier to learn about my grandparents. Why?" I ask.

He's about to respond, then changes his mind. Approaching, he kisses me good-night, then walks away quickly.

I remain at the door for a moment. I'm distressed by my father's revelation, hurt by his lack of understanding. I walk back into the house. Will my uncle talk to me tonight? I wonder, as I enter the dining room.

"What do you suppose is this 'surprise' Lozano mentioned?" Aunt Natalia is asking.

"A serenade," he says. Turning to me, he explains that it's the custom. "An old custom preserved in San Javier. After the serenade, one asks the musicians in, offers them drinks, and thanks them for their playing and singing."

"Oh, no, please! I cannot pronounce one more thank you," Monika bursts out, getting to her feet. "All day long I've been smiling, saying *gracias, gracias* for all the praises to Grandpa." She begins bowing, smiling exaggeratedly, imitating herself, causing her mother to laugh. "Sorry, I'm going to bed." She throws three kisses. Then, at the door, she says softly, "Dad, I was very proud of your speech."

"*Gracias*, Monika," he says, lowering his eyes, seemingly moved by his daughter's compliment.

Monika has probably barely reached her bedroom when we hear low voices and steps outside the house, then the tuning of instruments. A moment later, violins, flutes, guitars, and mandolins burst forth in a quick-rhythm piece.

No one in the room speaks. Aunt Natalia taps her hand softly on the table to the tempo of the music. For the second number, the musicians select a tune I vaguely recognize—a simple, repetitive melody. Then I know.

"This is the surprise!" Uncle Victor says. "Amazing how Lozano thought of everything." Looking at me, he adds, "The old man's song, my father's. He composed this for María Teresa and me—"

"I know about the song." I wipe my eyes brusquely, as if my tears are mosquitoes bothering me.

A man is singing, "*Porque mi camino es corto y estrecho/ Y el vuestro ancho y luminoso/ os contaré mis memorias, y escucharé vuestros sueños.*"

I watch my uncle, his chin trembling lightly. Aunt Natalia has placed her hand over his wrist.

"You're thinking about Mama, aren't you?" My tone is harsh, as if I'm ordering my uncle to agree with me promptly.

"I'm thinking of my father also," he says with a sadness that shocks me.

"It was for my birthday, my tenth birthday," he says softly. "He brought the musicians, like tonight, a serenade. Papa himself played the mandolin and sang the song." He pauses. "We were all in this room. Strange how certain images never go away. I still see María Teresa half sleeping, in Mama's lap."

"You mean my grandmother was not 'the crazy woman' then?"

Uncle Victor and his wife look at me, both frowning, then at each other. They're appalled that I'm making such a remark tonight. No one speaks for a moment. Then I say, "At least you told Monika and Lalita what happened. I had to come all the way to Colombia to learn the truth. Neither Mama nor Dad confided in me, their only child."

"Yesterday at brunch you told us, remember, Camila?" Aunt Natalia says. "You said that you had refused to listen to María Teresa's reminiscences, that you didn't want to hear more stories."

"That was at the end, Aunt Natalia, two years or so before she—Mama could have told me the truth about her family all those past years." I look at my uncle.

He doesn't answer. Perhaps he doesn't want to be interrupted as he listens to his father's song.

Aunt Natalia pours fresh coffee in his cup.

After a moment, he says, "Perhaps María Teresa saw that you were not ready for the truth. She was waiting for you to mature, Camila."

Aunt Natalia gets up and leaves the room quietly.

I bite my lips. Never before have I felt so misunderstood by those I love: my father, my uncle, Aunt Natalia. Never before have I felt so alone. Slowly I get to my feet. "Good night, Uncle Victor."

"You wanted me to answer your questions, Camila."

I shake my head. "You just answered . . . And Monika told me the whole story today. I also have to speak to you,

Uncle, to confess something I shouldn't have done. I'll write you a letter," I say on my way to the door.

"Don't go. We don't have to speak. Let's just sit here together in silence."

He's thinking about Mama, I say to myself, walking back to sit down. At this instant, I know he's seeing his sister in me. He wants to imagine that Mama is still alive, that they are together in this house, where all memories of their childhood turned to sadness. This "thoughtless house shrouded in solitude and silence, built for the convenience of one person," as he said yesterday. I have a sudden impulse to move closer and put my arms around my uncle.

The singer and musicians go on for some time with Grandfather's song. The melancholy music, my uncle's and my silence, the pale light from the ceiling lamp over the table give a dreamlike atmosphere to the room.

"You only wanted to love perfection, Camila." I give a start, as if my own unexpected thought has been uttered by someone else. Did Mama feel this way? I wonder. I loved my grandfather galloping on his horse under the moon . . . the giant of my dreams, emerging from a flaming sky, stepping over hills and trees, his hand extended toward me. Did I want to hear only the heroic and poetic about Grandfather? The music outside acquires a new significance, a heartbreaking nostalgia that fills my eyes with tears. I'm recalling one occasion when, coming home from school, I found Mama listening to her Colombian records, to this same piece the serenaders are playing now, *"El Cafetero"*—The Coffee Man. I noticed her eyes were red from crying. What had she been thinking . . . remembering? About her mother, Adelaida, from whom she was constantly separated, the woman who, in the town's rumor, was "*loca,* unable to take care of her children"? Yet that day I did not ask my mother why she had been crying. Was I afraid that she'd tell me a sad story, an answer that would destroy my fantasies about the giant and the moon?

"My father was a product of his era, his culture," Uncle Victor speaks at last. "He was a weak man, although he made everyone believe, himself mostly, that he was strong, someone always in control, *un hombre* in the absurd meaning of the word for his era and his pueblo. When he learned that my mother had been committed to an insane asylum, he rushed to her town. Her brothers refused to see him. At the asylum he was informed that his wife had died there, in that place where he, with the help of her brothers, had committed her. It was only then that he understood his action of that Easter Sunday. He returned to San Javier a destroyed man. He locked himself upstairs and rarely went out. He wanted to expiate his sin, his crime. Perhaps being the *hombre* he thought he was, he felt it was up to him, rather than God, to punish himself. That was the rumor around town, San Javier's last joke about Francisco Zamora.

"Mama died after María Teresa's wedding. I was in my last year of medical school in Madrid. Neither María Teresa nor I was informed about our mother's death. We kept receiving letters from Papa telling us that Mama was resting in a country place where she was receiving proper attention for her condition. This had been true for a while. You

175

see, after she returned with her brothers to her town, Mama was living in her family house with an old woman relative and her brother Juan, who was a bachelor. She was secluded, of course. Her brothers, my uncles, kept everything about their sister Adelaida a secret. It was only when I returned from Europe that Papa told me about the insane asylum and her death. He told me everything, including his lies, which were not to protect us, his children, but to preserve his reputation in this town." Uncle Victor doesn't speak for a moment. Perhaps the memory of his father telling him about his mother, her fate, is a grief for which he has no words, a pain belonging only to himself.

"But surely you and Mama knew about that Easter Sunday, didn't you?"

"Of course we knew. We were not in San Javier at the time. I was a senior at college, and María Teresa was in Bucaramanga. I recall that my first reaction, when I heard about it, was one of embarrassment. I also thought that it was perhaps a lie, a melodrama invented by San Javier's people. For a while I tried to wipe the whole thing from my mind. Then I became haunted by the memory of my mother and the images of that Sunday. I wanted to learn the truth, yet I knew no one in San Javier I could trust. I really had no friends in San Javier. Finally I decided to talk to Padre Roque. The priest was confused, ashamed that he, the pastor, did not intercede for his parishioner, a woman who was not *loca*. Padre Roque, like many in this town, was afraid of my father.

"For a while, to protect myself, I believed that perhaps after all, my mother had been mentally affected. The last time I saw her she had tiptoed into my room in the middle of the night, whispering about a hidden road, a river to cross. She was concealing a pistol she had stolen from my father's collection in her robe. Mama was speaking about escaping, leaving my father. Was I too young to understand? Or was I too selfish, thinking only of my own future, my career, my father's promise to send me to Europe? These considerations will never go away."

"And Mama?"

"She also knew about that Sunday. She was very protected, living with Aunt Chinca and her husband. The version given to María Teresa was, of course, Aunt Chinca's. Since she was my father's sister, she was convinced that Mama was *loca*, that my father, poor thing, had been forced to send his wife back to her family home, in a city where she was surrounded by the medical attention she needed. To protect my sister, I helped María Teresa believe Aunt Chinca's story. It was only later, before you were born, that María Teresa, like you, became obsessed to learn the truth about our mother. For a while, she was bitter and resentful toward me. Being the girl, she was helpless. I could have done something to help our mother. That was her complaint. Strangely, she never said anything against Papa.

"María Teresa and Bill came to San Javier. It was here in this room one night that I told her about my conversation with Papa. I told her everything. After that, we remained here for hours, silent. We didn't need to describe our feelings. But we didn't tell Papa that he had made us orphans, that nothing he had done for us as a father in the past,

177

nothing he could do for us in the future, would take away the pain of our mother, her life and death in that place . . ." He pauses for a moment. "We told him that it wasn't his fault. We wanted our father to live his last years in peace, to be sure of our affection. He died a recluse gnawed by remorse."

"How could Mama—Did she read the letters I found in a leather box upstairs?"

"Those letters should have remained there, Camila! Those letters do not belong to you. At least you could have waited to ask me before taking possession of them."

"I'm sorry, Uncle. I'll return them to you before I leave."

"I hid the letters from your mother."

I'm relieved, glad that Mama didn't see the letters. "Grandfather died without ever hearing a reproach from either of his children," I murmur.

"It wasn't our place to judge him, as María Teresa repeated. God alone could judge him. Or a perfect, flawless being could condemn him. Do you know that person, Camila?" He looks at me for a moment.

I look away. Then my eyes turn toward Grandfather's portrait. You took refuge upstairs, where you could conceal your remorse. You wanted to hide your tears, what you, no doubt, considered your weakness. Yet in spite of my silent reproaches, I feel pity for my grandfather. No, I rebel immediately. Those are not my feelings. Perhaps tonight, in this room, I am momentarily his daughter, my mother. Perhaps one day I'll find forgiveness in my heart, like my mother.

* * *

On the plane, my father asks, "Did Victor answer all your questions, Camila?"

"I have no questions anymore, Dad. Thank you for allowing me to come to San Javier."

"Matesa was going to tell you everything. She was waiting for you to be ready."

"I know," I murmur, as my father moves to embrace me.

It's not until I'm under the sky of my country, as the plane descends, that I think of the house in Connecticut. I see myself entering, walking into the kitchen first, then along the hall and in and out of the rooms. Today I'll go to the garden, to the spot where I found Mama that afternoon last October. There, near the roses, with my mother's presence within me, is the beginning of the journey that lies ahead for me, the woman, returning from San Javier.

ABOUT THE AUTHOR

Lyll Becerra de Jenkins is the author of the widely acclaimed *The Honorable Prison,* which won the Scott O'Dell Award for Historical Fiction and has been translated into many languages. Ms. Jenkins' short stories have appeared in periodicals and books throughout the world, including the *New Yorker,* the *New York Times,* and *Best American Short Stories.* She teaches writing at Fairfield University in Connecticut.

Ms. Jenkins was born and raised in Colombia. She now lives in Monroe, Connecticut, with her husband, John. They have five children and two grandchildren.